MARKED
Tales of S.T.A.N.G.E.

K.L. Patrick

To Nanny and Dave, I miss you everyday.
I hope we've made you proud.

Acknowledgements

Sometimes life gets in the way of things, and I find myself feeling down. Yet, at the same time, I find hope in the people I have become friends with throughout my writing journey.

First and foremost, I must thank my wife, Haley. Without her encouragement of my work, I wouldn't be here, and I wouldn't be writing. She listens to my ideas, shares my hopes and dreams, and fills me with an endless love. Even when I am speaking about silly ideas that go nowhere. Without her encouragement I wouldn't be half the writer I am today. I love you, Haley.

Momma, again your love and support always means the world. You believed Devin and I could do anything, and I hope we make you proud. Without you and Nanny Hilda, we wouldn't be who we are today.

Dylan, your support means everything. We have been friends for so long that nothing I do surprises you anymore. I hope you continue to enjoy my work. Without our video game talks I doubt my ideas would be anywhere near as interesting.

To Ian Geilen, Jim Donohue, Jules Terry, Trevor Woods, The Haunted Minds Discord Crew, and Chaos Scribes. Your encouragement is where the universe of these stories comes from. Thank you for reading my work, commenting on my ideas, and making me laugh. The Three Forks universe wouldn't exist without you.

To Lisa Wood, Nick Roberts, and everyone else who has mentored me along the way. I am a better writer because of each of you. Thank you not just for the encouragement, but everything you have done, and continue to do for me. I hope to pay it forward as well.

To Devin, thank you for helping with the chapter illustrations, it means the world. You are so talented. Believe in yourself buddy, and the world will too.

To Savannah Fischer, thank you for the cover and the formatting. It means the world to me, my friend.

To Jyl Glenn, thank you for all your help throughout the process, I cannot put into words how much it all means. Your kindness means the world to me, and I cannot wait to share more of my work with you.

Lastly, thanks to you, my readers. Without you, nothing would come from this odd, country boys work without you.

The Basement

The building was demolished, as if it had been picked up and tossed through the trees into the darkness of life. The man sighed as he rolled his cigarette and lit it. John Nelson didn't think stuff like this could happen anymore. But it did, with an increasing frequency, and he was the one sent to the middle of Butt Fuck Nowhere tucked between Floyd and Franklin County, high above the little valley community of Callaway.

Dammit Silas, this should've been you. But of course, Simon came first. He didn't even say where he was going. John let out the smoke from within his lungs. It pulsed through the damp air in front of him. Of course, it had to be raining as well. He really didn't want to be here, but seeing as he was available and able to go up against whatever this thing was, of course, he was the one who would be brought here. Magic powers or not, death still haunted him. A face swam up to the surface–Marie, all she did for him, the president's daughter. Well, now former president.

John's skills were perfect for situations like these. Investigating was second nature, and if he found a clue, it wouldn't take long to solve the case. John scanned the ground looking for anything that could help him. *Ahhh.* A book lay face down on the ground. It was black Moleskine; quite a nice-looking book to be honest. One that could easily be worth a hundred dollars.

He flipped it open and its rough pages nicked at his skin. He had opened it from the back. The book seemed to be mostly empty, except for a handful of entries. *Better to go with the first.* The journal seemed to belong to a Jack Basham, and he had written this three days ago. *What could've happened?* John struggled with the knarred cursive, but it came forward quickly, reaching into his mind, and creating the world around him.

July 19th, 1990 8:00 A.M.

Never go to the basement. That was the first rule they gave me when I arrived at the orphanage. Saint Teresa's was a towering place, way off in the woods of Virginia. A place that shouldn't have existed nestled deep in the mountains as if it were hidden from prying eyes. The building was gothic and old. I have no clue how old it is, because it was so different from every building I had seen in my life, with the crumbling stone that lined its walls. Shoot, it was dang creepy. Towers rose to either side like a castle. The stone was old and cracking. Vines lined the edges of the orphanage. Its windows stared out sightlessly toward the road that became its driveway. Trees surrounded the property, and honestly, the forest was spookier than the building itself. The woods were always dark. Darker than dark. So ink-black that when you looked into them, you were sure you would never return. Part of me wondered if something lurked within them. I still think something might, but that's another story. I gulped and walked toward the big wooden doors. The Gargoyles watched my approach. They reminded me of the ones that lined the church across from my parents' house, a place I could never return to. The place where my heart was shattered, and I would never, ever, be the same.

I wished I could go back there. To the warmth of that house. To the love of my parents. But they were gone and I was alone. Fear filled me and my arms shook. I spun around, ready to run back to the cab that had brought me. It was gone. I thought I could barely make it out in the distance kicking dust high into the sky. I guess he didn't want to be out here either. Shoot, he'd said as much on the ride.

"We don't come out here, kid. It ain't safe. There are stories, yah know. Stories of the place being possessed," He stopped for a moment, pulling his straw hat down as we drove. I wanted to smile at the man, but the look on his face was one of concern. The man even pulled a little bottle out of the pocket of his bib overalls, popped the cap, and pushed it to his lips. At that moment I thought he was thirsty, but now I know he probably had alcohol hidden within it. Thinking back, I could see some of that amber liquid trickle onto his grey beard. I can't blame him. I have whiskey here at my desk, to make me forget the screaming that echoes through the night. The screaming that fills my heart with nothing but dread, but we aren't there yet. No, not yet.

"They say the nuns built that place for a reason. Maybe it's the grace of God, but here in the mountains of Franklin, I cain't think of a real reason they would build the place there. It could be for Jesus. They are Catholic after all...but why it became an orphanage, I will never know." He continued.

I bounced in the back seat, afraid of what may be coming, but I was holding on to this man's every word. I didn't know what to say, and every time I did, he interrupted, making me forget the words that sat on my tongue. I was so young, and so scared.

"In the end I guess they might've wanted to help the kids here. A lot end up in houses like this, or broken homes. I know I did back in the day. You'll find out soon enough. What happened? Your parents drink too much? They druggies?"

I went to answer, but he again interrupted me.

"It doesn't matter. You're just a kid, I'm sorry."

We bounced down the gravel road faster than I would've liked. The man was mad to be driving how he was on a dirt road. I closed my eyes for just a moment, as I was starting to feel a little sick. Before I knew it, he slammed on the brakes and left me in the dust in this place that wasn't quite *right*. The surrounding woods seemed to pull at me, as if they wanted me. It was an option; I could get away and be a wild man free in the Appalachian Mountains. But the thought of going into them alone broke me. I made my way back to the gigantic front door and knocked. The sound echoed deep through the chamber. The echo was so loud I could hear it outside where I stood.

No one came.

What was I going to do, just enter? There was no way I could do that. So, I knocked again and again. I knocked for so long that my hand was beginning to hurt. But...

No one came.

There was only one thing to do. My hands shook so hard that I had to hold them tight to stop them. I got them under control rather quickly and turned back to the door. As I reached out to the door, the shakes returned. *Why was I so scared?* I didn't know it yet, but I definitely had a good reason. One that haunts me to this very day.

A sound pulled John from his reading. He was sitting on a big stone, trying to figure out what may have happened. What could the sound have been? As far as he could tell, he was alone. Only the dead accompanied him. He looked into the woods in time to see a tentacle disappear into the darkness. *Of course he is watching. Waiting to take me back.* He pushed it from his mind. That was his future, this was his now.

A brick fell somewhere in the distance. He pulled the cigarette from his mouth and knocked the ash into the wind. He walked for a moment, book still in hand. John passed around the corner, where he found a hole busting through a wall. Whatever had done this was big. Black hair lined the side of the hole.

"Odd," he muttered as he approached it. John picked up the hair and shuddered. The hair was stiff and bristly. *Where could this have come from?* Whatever it was, it wasn't human.

"Help!" A distant voice said. Someone was here, and pain wracked every wail. As if they had been completely destroyed.

John turned around. "Hello?"

"Help!" The voice came from the other side of a rock. John tossed the hair on the ground and made his way around the other rubble. A boy lay in a pool of blood. A huge piece of rubble pinned his legs to the ground. "Shit," John said, tossing his cigarette to the ground. He knelt down next to the boy.

"What happened?" John asked.

"Monster." was all the boy was able to get out. His light blue eyes were fading; his blonde hair was now a mop of blood. *That's why he's here.* There was nothing he could do. He watched as the boy took his last breath. It was shuttering, terrible, and a sadness fell across him. No matter how many times he saw someone die, it was always hard. John's chest tightened. *This boy is too young to have to go see him, what a waste.* Why was it always so hard? A tear slid down his cheek. Especially watching a boy of maybe twelve pass through the veil. John stood and waited for it to happen. It usually didn't take long.

After about five minutes, the boy sat up and pulled himself to his feet, leaving the body behind. The boy looked down, then looked at John.

"What did you do?" The boy asked as he stared at his own body.

"Nothing, son." John looked down. This was the hardest part. Talking to the recently deceased was always a drain on him. "What's your name son?"

"Corey," he said, and smiled. Probably unable to believe he was standing again.

"What happened? What was the monster."

The boy thought for a moment. "It was a s—" Something black shot out of the ground. "What?"

"I'm so sorry. So, so, sorry." John wished he could save the boy, but this was the way all the dead went. *He* came for them all in the end.

The tentacles grabbed the boy, wrapping around him till they covered his entire body.

"Help!" He screamed as he was pulled into the earth.

"Every time." It didn't get any easier, no matter how many times he saw it, and he couldn't get any answers out of the boy—Corey. No matter, he had other methods.

John reached into his jacket pocket and pulled out a vial. He bent down to the boy's body. First, he pushed the boy's eyes closed. Then he filled the vial with blood. It would come in use later, if the book didn't have the answers. The ritual was too risky without a second person, and John would prefer to avoid doing it if he could.

John leaned back against the wall and let out a sigh before pulling out another cigarette. With how tall he was, it was so easy to see over the rubble. He perched the book on the pile of crumbled rock in front of him. *Come on Jack, give me something.*

January 19th, 1990 12:00 P.M.

I thought I could write the origins all in one go but it takes its toll on me. Reliving the memories, even the early ones of my arrival, are too much. So, I had to take a break, not that anyone will read this, but maybe getting it off my chest will bring me forgiveness, and forgiveness is all I need.

As I pushed through the door, it squeaked, announcing my entrance. I had quite a bit of trouble with it because the door was so heavy. So incredibly heavy.

A vast chamber shadowed by stairs met me. I stood there, looking at my feet. I was unsure of what to do besides look at the stone floor. There had to be someone to greet me, *right?* To show me around? To get me settled? Yet the room was empty, the only sound was of my own breathing. I must have stood for hours before someone saw me. A nun ran to me, smiling.

"How long 'ave you been here, dear?" She asked.

I shrugged, not wanting to talk, wishing this nightmare would end. Wanting to be back home. With mom and dad. In a world I knew. But something in the woman's kind eyes gave me pause. Even as young as I was, she must've seen the fear in my eyes, how lost I was. Because she squatted down and took my hand in hers. The deep green of her eyes peered into mine.

"You're going to be safe here." She smiled.

It took away all my fears, all my sadness... all my hurt. Even the fear that came from the woods, and what the cab driver had said. She took it all away in an instant, and for the first time in a long time I smiled. A full, loving smile.

"Come with me. We didn't know you were coming or we would've had someone to welcome you." She smiled again, and a warmth washed over me. She held out a hand and I took it.

She ushered me upstairs, past a ton of other boys, and into what would be my room. I shared it with one other boy. His name was Michael. He became my best friend. The nun turned to leave, and I jumped up.

"This is your room now. Don't worry, I'll see you at dinner." With that she was gone, and I was left alone to take in the room. I sat my bag on my bed. All my worldly belongings were in one place now. The room was darker and colder than the room I had at my former 'home.' It was as if I was dropped into what I imagined a prison cell would look like, except the room had a wooden floor. There wasn't even a window in the room. My heart dropped. How was I going to live here in this place? To be alone? I touched the steel bed, and it was just as cold. That's what my life was going to be. Cold and broken. I walked to the stone wall and touched it, and my hand almost instantly froze.

When I turned around, a boy stood in the doorway, and I laughed. He was taller than me, with jet black hair, his clothes were too big, and he looked oddly goofy. He laughed silently at me and smiled a buck-tooth smile.

"Hi," I said, and walked toward him. "Are you my roommate?"

He waved and nodded, before running forward and grabbing my hand. He took me to his side of the room, where he had a small trunk. *Michael* was written on it. He pointed at it, and then himself.

"You're Michael?" I asked.

He nodded. A smile formed on his face again. Suddenly, he popped under his bed and pulled out a checkers set. He pointed at it then pointed at me.

"Yea."

He poured out the box and set it up. We played till dinner, and I don't know why, but we became fast friends.

There were many rules; this was something I learned very quickly without any thought or any real reason. I wasn't a bad kid, but I found a way to learn all the rules firsthand. Such as going to bed at eight, not fighting the other kids, and most importantly, never going to the basement. I figured it was a safety thing. Turns out it wasn't, but hindsight is 20/20. When the same nun from the day before came and gave me a tour down the old creaking hallways, she brought me to a singular door.

"Jack, you must never mess with this door. No one goes into the basement." It was old, and the wood was cracked, like with most of the orphanage. The dull brass of the doorknob glittered, and there was a lock above it. A dead bolt, to be exact. I tried popping it multiple times in that first year, but it was too sturdy.

"Why?" I asked as children do, and the nun grabbed me by both shoulders and looked me straight in the eyes.

"It's not safe. Never try to get in. Okay?"

I nodded and took in the door. She grabbed my hand and walked me away from it. I couldn't help but glance over my shoulder where, through the keyhole, something shone. Something deep in that blackness. Just like with the woods, it had a pull on me. It still has a pull on me as I write this. I can only hope I don't do anything stupid and release the beast within. We went around the corner leading to a cafeteria-like place, it was just a stone room we ate in, the moment my eyes left the door, it was like a string was cut, and I was free. Yet my mind still focused on that door, cracked and splintered as it was, there was something important about it. But I couldn't put a finger on it. God, I wish that I could've stopped thinking about the door, maybe life could've been different.

For the rest of the day nothing much happened, but I still couldn't help thinking about the door. Then the night came and everything about the orphanage changed. It became darker, and colder, something was different. Something that was so different from the warm house I knew as a kid, that it almost broke my mind. How could a building change so much? As my room filled with darkness, I pulled the covers around me. Then I heard the muttering beneath the floorboards.

Late at night, if you didn't go to bed at the right time, you could hear a grotesque muttering from underneath the floors. Or I could hear it... Michael could too, or at least he claimed he did despite being mute. He would point to the floors and shake.

"Free me," a voice said. Michael and I would tremble in our beds, heads covered with blankets to keep from screaming, to keep from seeing, hearing, but the sound went on. The lady who ran the place would have beaten us if she heard us. She wasn't as nice as the nun who greeted me when I got to the orphanage. She was old, almost cronelike, every little thing you did would piss her off. She would say it was not godlike. Even her light green eyes would strike fear into me in an instance. Her name was Mother Muriel, and she was the scourge of my existence for most of my life. Until that night, that damn night, but I'm getting ahead of myself.

As the months went on, the muttering got louder, and Michael and I slowly realized we were the only ones who could hear it. When we mentioned it to the other kids, they would just say.

"What're yah talking about? I ain't heard nothin'." Important note, the orphanage being in rural Appalachia meant a lot of kids didn't read and write. A lot could, but a lot couldn't. Especially in 1930. So, none of us were considered educated. Over the past sixty years I realize that might not have been the truth. Part of me wonders if they could hear it and were just pretending. It would've made perfect sense but either way Michael and I couldn't read either, but a kid named Johnny could.

We got a book on lock picking, I can't remember where from, maybe from one of our biannual outings to town. The orphanage would round us all up, and we would go down to the tiny town of Floyd. There we would eat, and just have a great time, but tried not to cause trouble. Mother Muriel was always watching us, and in the end, it could be too much for the nuns, and someone would get in trouble, and we would go back up the hill. We would have to walk all the way back up the mountain. I reckon Johnny must've hidden the book under his shirt or something. It was the only way I could think of that he would've gotten ahold of the book.

Johnny read it to us, and we all practiced. It took a while for Michael and me to get the hang of it, but after weeks of practice, we were confident enough to go into the basement. We needed to know what was down there. What could make all those sounds? Neither of us could sleep. So, of course, being kids, we needed answers. What was plaguing our nights? And why just us?

We asked Johnny if he wanted to join us. He did, and we were ready to go down there that night. I think he was the only one who believed us. Or maybe he just enjoyed mischief. I mean he was the one who would lead us to the kitchen at night to steal food. He was also always picking on the other kids, but he was a good friend. I can still see his bright red hair and gap tooth grin today. I hope he is doing okay. I wish I could've found him after I was old enough to leave the orphanage, but I never did and suspect I never will. But I am getting off topic again. The day we agreed to go down turned out to be the day a family came.

Those were the most exciting days. All of us wanted nothing more than to be adopted. But so often we wouldn't get the chance, especially since I was going on thirteen at this point. Every time I was overlooked, in my heart I knew I would never have a real family again. Usually, the younger kids were the ones who got adopted. Usually those under five. Johnny, Michael and I would never get a second look, but this family was different. They talked to all of us. I wanted a family. I wanted one so bad. I wanted out of this place and couldn't help getting excited. The feeling, and of possibly being loved by someone again was almost intoxicating, and I couldn't help but smile.

"What's your name?" the mother asked. She was beautiful, with deep red hair and such kind eyes. She was tall, way taller than me even at thirteen, and had a smile that filled my heart with joy. I could only wonder if this lady was going to be my mom. Oh, how I would've loved for that to happen.

"Jack," I said, looking down at my feet. I couldn't bring myself to look her in the eyes. She was so beautiful and seeing as the nuns were the only women we saw daily, I was a tad bit nervous.

The muttering started then. It was the first time I had ever heard it during the day. I shook my head, hoping it would go away. But it didn't, it only got louder, and louder. To the point I wanted to scream.

Free me.

"You okay, honey?"

I nodded. She ruffled my hair and turned to talk to Johnny. I glanced at Michael. His face contorted in a way I only saw at night. The father was trying to talk to Michael, and the nearest nun had to explain that Michael was mute. The rumor I heard was that he had seen something horrible. One rumor said it was his sister committing suicide. Others said it was his parents' death.

Which wasn't too different from me. I saw the car crash that took my parents in all its bloody glory. For some reason the muttering brought the memory back. The one from the day my parents died.

July 20th, 1990 11:30 A.M.

I didn't want to relieve this part, and have been putting it off since yesterday, but I needed to do something, anything. To keep the screaming from entering my very soul. Thus, I return to that night.

We were driving home from getting ice cream. Mine slipped from my hand and had fallen to the floorboard. I cried and cried. My mom and dad had turned around to try to calm me down.

Even sixty years later, I still remember every detail. I wish I could've let it go, but I can't. I just couldn't remember what my parents were saying. They were so kind. I hope I have lived up to their expectations, but I'm sure I haven't.

Through the windshield, I saw the truck... a coal truck. Mom had drifted into its lane. The horn honked. My dad yelled something and grabbed the steering wheel, trying to cut to the right. The truck clipped our rear end.

We spun and flipped. We rolled and rolled and slammed into something. There wasn't such a thing as seat belts yet, so I should've died. I could never say how I survived, just that when I opened my eyes, there was blood everywhere. Mom and Dad's heads were in the back seat with me... It's still hard to think about. I loved them so much, and they were gone. My memories have even faded into oblivion, yet I still remember their deaths, and I know I will continue to remember just that until I meet them in heaven. That is if God lets me enter after what I've done.

I wonder if that's why Michael and I could hear that damn voice. Maybe it was because we had seen death firsthand. Experienced it, tasted the blood, smelled the smells firsthand. Could that be why we were the only ones who could hear the disembodied voice? I still wonder that to this day. Here in my office, I can still hear the voice. Screaming, and yelling trying to find a way free. But there is only one way, and I have the key.

Michael and I both cowered against the wall and watched while the family took away Johnny. I couldn't help but smile for him, despite the terror I felt at that moment. My friend was now free. I just wish we could've gone with him. It would've stopped everything. He made it out. Something I never managed to do. He never got to pick that lock.

Progressively, the sounds increased in volume until they became a screaming, instead of a muttering. Night after night we lost sleep, to the point where we couldn't keep going. I began to fall asleep in any classes they had, and missed things, because the light was the only time we ever had a reprieve. After long enough, Michael and I had to do something, even if he couldn't speak, I could see the fear in his eyes. The lack of sleep that lined his face. We had to do something, and we had to do it soon.

A scream echoed through the woods. Louder than John had ever heard. He jumped, reaching for his gun. There was something out there in the dark. Something that had to be what caused this. The only issue was he couldn't pinpoint where it had come from. The woods were vast in this part of the country, and whatever the 'monster' was, it could be anywhere.

John walked around through all the rubble and found two other bodies, one looked like it had been bitten in half, while the other had been torn limb from limb. *So, there were three boys.* Too bad their blood was too old to use, or he could see what had happened to them.

The last body was on the edge of the rubble almost in the grass the kid had almost gotten away. *Dammit,* his eyes moved from each boy to the old man at the center of the rubble. The man was dressed in what must have been reverend garb, which made no sense because the orphanage had been Catholic, even if the nuns were long gone. He had been dead for a while as well. John lifted the book. So, this was who had been writing in it. John was still no closer to what that thing may be. Another scream echoed through the mountains. There wasn't much time.

July 20th, 10:00 P.M.

April 12, 1937, was the night we went down there–the night that everything changed. The day was a normal one, but I was anxious the whole time. I was lost in my own head, not paying attention to anyone.

I was about to head to lunch when a hand grabbed my shoulder. I jumped out of my skin; afraid it was one of the other kids. At this point they hated me and Michael and were always looking for an excuse to bully us. I did my best to always avoid them, and they had never come to me, usually I was the one to cross their paths.

I clenched my fists as I turned around, only to see those kind eyes. Alice. It was Alice. At the time I still didn't know her name, but she was the same lady who had greeted me when I came in as a kid.

"You okay, Jack?" She asked. The concern in her voice was almost palpable; her face lined with a frown. It was the first time I had ever seen her frown. Ever. She was scared for me, and I still to this day don't know why. Maybe she knew what I would do that night? Or maybe she just cared that much. Either way she was there, looking me in the eye. In those eyes I saw fear.

"I'm okay," I lied. She didn't need to know I wasn't okay, and I may never be okay again. The screams in the night have only gotten worse over the years, leaving me wondering why I am still here. Why am I still protecting this place, but if it gets out? Sorry I'm getting ahead of myself again. Lord help me, I wish I could believe he was still here with us. But God has abandoned this place and left me here to watch. Watching is exactly what I do. Waiting for the moment where it all changes again.

The night we went down there was especially bad. The screaming was unbearable, even covering our ears didn't help. It was as if the screaming was in our very brains. There was a scraping under the floor. Which made no sense, our room was on the third floor, so there should've been nothing below us except another room.

The moon twinkled off the headboards of our beds. The comfort I once felt from the moon was gone and I lay awake waiting for the moment of our pilgrimage. Michael and I couldn't even talk to each other. That's how loud the sounds were coming from the basement. Not that he would've talked anyway, but you see my point. We opened our door. Both dressed in our pajamas. Michael was a bigger boy, and his bottoms didn't cover his legs well. We often had to wear old clothes. They wouldn't get us any new ones. The only kindness we saw was from Alice. Other than that, we were alone.

His mass of black hair sprung about as we walked down the hall. We tried to avoid all the creaks of the old building, something we had mastered from our nighttime trips. All of it was preparation for this moment. We made our way to the stairs and looked down. A faint light crossed the floor. It might have been another nun, but we never truly found out. We stood waiting. Holding our breath. When no one came, we proceeded.

We tiptoed down the stairs and the screams just got louder.

"Help me," something said. The sound still brings me chills. By the time we were at the forbidden door, our ears felt as if they may burst. Michael looked at me and nodded. I pulled the bobby pin out; I squirreled it away from one of the girls and straightened it out. I inserted it into the lock and did exactly what John had taught me.

My head pounded from the screams that had been going on for hours. It kept getting louder, and I thought I would lose consciousness, when finally, the lock clicked open.

I pushed the door open, and the screams stopped. The sudden silence shocked me.

"What the hell?" I said as I stared down into the darkness. I could see the stairs, but not where they went. As if the darkness had thickened. A stench like rotten eggs and feces punched my nostrils. I turned to Michael, and he wasn't there. Where had he gone so fast? Michael was halfway down the stairs.

"Michael," I said. He stopped and turned around and waved at me. "Michael, come back." He shook his head *no.* Something in the darkness moved into the light of the stairs. It was almost like a spider but had a giant human mouth in the center of its head. Black fur covered it. It had no eyes. Michael turned and screamed as the thing bit down upon him. That scream still haunts me.

The scream was cut off in an instant as the blood exploded from his lower half. Michael's legs still stood as if they didn't know the brain had just been devoured. After a moment, they fell. Michael's bones crunched as the thing ate him. Blood rained down the stairs, covering the thing. Glistening it in a gory bath of crimson.

I knew I had to run and relock the door, but I couldn't move. Its legs thumped against the steps in the darkness. It was coming for me. I grabbed the door and slammed it. The sound echoed throughout the whole orphanage.

Doors opened above me, and the screaming resumed. The monster slammed against the door as I tried to hold it shut. I yelled at the top of my lungs for help. A nun arrived. It was Alice, she jumped into action and helped hold the door shut. The screams got louder, and Alice trembled as she searched for the right key. After what felt like an eternity, she found it and slid it into the lock. The loudest scream of them all came. The walls shook around us. Everyone's eardrums must've ruptured, I know mine did. Alice slumped against the door holding her chest. Something warm and wet ran from my ears.

"I said never to open the door," Alice said. Pain creased her face. She gripped her chest. "The monster must not escape... We must guard... That is... our duty." She slumped over—dead. I stood over her body as the other children arrived. All in shock. All staring at me, their eyes told me what I believed. That it was all my fault.

After that day, I knew I couldn't leave. I had started something, and its screams still enchant me. Still haunts me. Even after my hearing went, it still broke through. There are no longer kids here, there is only me, and the darkness I must hide. Is that a knock? The building still plays tricks on me. Lord help me.

John almost had the ritual ready. He needed to see what the thing was, and his only option was through the ritual. God, he hated this part. *It* was already close, and he didn't want to bring it closer with the ritual. If only he could've got more info from the book. He needed to know how it got out. If he could learn that maybe he could stop the thing or at least reimprison it. It was definitely from beyond the common human know how. But was it from beyond, or just a captured being from the earth? Was it eldritch, or of our realm? Shoot, it could even be one of the Lovecraft's 'Old Ones,' for all John knew.

On the ground lay a spiral in salt, perfect, unending. Disappearing into the rubble on the other side of him. John stood over the center and poured out the vial of blood.

"Enascor!" He yelled, and a light flashed brightly, lighting everything around him. Red filled the spiral and it shot upward into the sky. The light was so bright John couldn't see for a moment. Then the dust of the salt started to take form, showing a huge wooden door and three figures standing in the redness. He could make out Corey, but the other two dead teens he didn't recognize. One had long hair pulled tight in a ponytail. The problem with blood magic is you can't tell the color of anything. The other was nearly bald, which was odd for someone so young, they were pushing against each other, before Corey finally lifted a hand, and knocked against the door three times.

"I told you no one lives here," Corey said as he turned around. His friends Cliff and Billy had convinced him to come all the way up here.

"Are you saying you don't want to drink in this spooky place? It'll be fun! And I already have the beer." Cliff held up the case of beer. "Dad's special. He loves these things."

"You sure your dad ain't going to miss it?" Billy asked, as he held the sleeves of his jacket, pulling at them. Billy was the type who wore a jacket year-round no matter the season, to the point where Corey had never seen him without one.

"Nah, he's too drunk to miss this."

"It couldn't be the opposite, could it?" Corey asked. "Let's get out of here." Hoping his friends would agree to leave. But at that very moment the door opened. Standing within was a tall man, he was older, older than any man Corey had ever seen. Tuffs of white hair appeared above his mostly bald head. A smile crossed his face for a moment, as if the man hadn't seen anyone in a very, very, long time. Corey thought the man must've realized he was smiling because as quick as it happened it was gone.

"What y'all want." He asked in a gravely, deep voice. It was so deep it even shook Corey's chest.

"Hey, old man, we thought this place was abandoned," Cliff said with a smile.

The old man didn't return it. A sadness crossed through his eyes.

"Almost is," the old man said. "Once I'm gone there will be no one else to watch over the place." The man's hand shook as he spoke. "Y'all should get back down the mountain." The man pretended to be glancing into the sky. "Night's coming."

"Can't we see inside?" Billy asked.

"Yeah, can't we?" Cliff said, pushing out his bottom lip.

Corey hated when his friends did this, they acted so much younger than they actually were. Which made him mad. Corey could feel that anger welling up within him. Being the quiet one he was always along for the ride with those two. They always used the same trick to convince him.

Shoot it's how they convinced him to come up here in the first place. A part of Corey hated them for it.

"That's a big door," Corey said absentmindedly. He knew they wanted him to join in their game, but he refused to do so. Ever.

The man smiled at them and slammed the door. They heard a soft click, as he locked it back in place.

"Damn, that didn't go as planned," Cliff said, leaning against the stone behind him.

"What did you really expect?" Billy asked. "That he would just let us come in?"

"Can't we just go home?" Corey shot in, hopeful his friends had had enough of their fun. They could go to the pizza place and enjoy the rest of their Tuesday night. Especially since it was summer break.

"Think there's another way in?" Billy said, completely ignoring Corey like always.

"Let's see," Cliff said, kicking off the wall, and taking off around the side of the building.

"Guys." They were gone. They never asked his opinion. Never ever. "Wait," Corey sighed and chased them around the side of the building.

The friends made their way around the building with a speed Corey didn't think possible. The cold stone was their guide. It towered over the boys.

"Wait up," Corey called after them, but once again they didn't listen to him. It was as if he didn't exist within their minds, unless they needed something, and he was getting tired of it. So dang tired. It was even his car that they came in. *They never appreciate me.* When he came around the corner his friends were stopped, looking at something on the ground. Or at least on ground level.

"What is it guys?" Corey asked as he approached. Then he saw it. In front of them was a small hole in the foundation where the stones were falling away. Deep within was a darkness, dark and deep. Deeper than they had ever seen.

"Think that's the basement?" Cliff asked with a goofy smile across his face.

"We might be able to get in yet," Billy said, giving Cliff a high five. "Maybe the old man has some alcohol down there. That would be super cool."

It wouldn't be cool. But they were already pulling at the rocks, so there was really no way he could make his friends stop what they were doing. Instead, he just watched as they pulled out chunks of rock until the opening was big enough for them to fit through. All of them were skinny so it really didn't take long at all.

Corey kept looking over his shoulder, hoping that the old man hadn't come out and found them. If he did, they would need to run for the car before he called the cops, but there was no sound. Only silence, not even a bid was singing. It was as if the world had stopped. Fog like hot breath frothed out of the hole in front of them. But it was summer? How could it be that cold in there? It couldn't be possible. Instead of being scared Corey leaned forward as his friend leaned back.

It was as if he was entranced by whatever was coming from there. Corey knelt down looking into the darkness. Watching the cold air spew out.

"Is it possible for a basement to be that cold?" He asked. His voice trembled.

"No," Billy said. "Not at all."

"Unless it is because of these old cobblestones," Cliff chimed in. He kicked the wall and another rock fell, and the hole had become a mouth.

Corey looked at it as if it was hungry. Then pulled the flashlight out of his pocket that he had brought in case it got dark while they were out. He leaned forward, and as he did, he heard his friend's giggle.

A foot planted firmly into his back, and with a slight amount of forward pressure Corey lost his balance and slid headfirst into the hole.

Corey hit the ground hard and bounced lightly. Something sticky covered his body from head to toe. He touched it and it stretched off like gum in front of him, only slightly more silky.

Where am I? The darkness was all consuming down here, filling the whole area in front and around him. His friends laughed loudly above him.

"Dudes, give me a light," Corey yelled, before clapping his hand over his mouth. He didn't want the old man to hear him. That would be a disaster, especially now that he was down here in the darkness. Who knows what the man kept in the basement, it could even be dead bodies. *No, that's your horror movie obsession talking. He seemed like a perfectly normal old man.*

His mind was still running a thousand miles per hour when Cliff and Billy slid in. Except they came down feet first.

"What was that guys?" Corey asked. He tried not to be too mad about it, but it irritated him that they did crap like this to him.

"Calm down, it was just a joke," Cliff said, punching Corey in the shoulder.

"I could've broken my neck."

"But you didn't."

Cory took a step closer. "I could've."

"But you didn't, so we're good."

"Guys look." Billy called from behind them. He had a flashlight and was shining it around the room. The floor was lined with a silky white substance. *Is that a spider web?* Corey reached down and picked up some of the cobwebs.

"How can it be this dirty?" Corey asked as he wiped the webs on his pants.

"Old man must not have been down here in a good long while," Billy said. His voice tremored slightly. Corey was sure he was trying not to be scared.

"Maybe he's too old to come down here!" Cliff said and laughed.

Why is he always so cold hearted?

A rancid wind blew past them causing them all to gag.

"We need to get out of here," Corey whispered.

"What's that smell?" Cliff asked.

"Don't know, but it ain't fun." Billy covered his nose. "There are stairs. Let's go." He ran forward toward the stairs and clomped up them.

Corey's body numbed with fear. *It's only a dirty basement. Why are we so scared?*

They clomped up the stairs and slammed into the door. Corey's heart jumped in his chest, as if it was trying to escape. Something echoed behind them, and they slammed into the door over and over. After the third hit, the lock broke and they fell out onto the ground. The door swung in front of them.

Cliff jumped to his feet and slammed the door shut. The sound of it echoed through the corridor in front of them.

It was vast, taller than anything the boys had ever seen.

"Woah! This place is crazy," Corey muttered.

They walked into the dusty corridor, the vaulted ceilings filling them with a dread they had never felt before. The orphanage was insane.

"He lives here all by himself?" Billy asked as he touched the wall in front of him. "It's so cold."

"Yea." Corey shivered. *How is this possible?* He didn't know a room could be this cold.

"I guess they ain't got heat," Billy said, "And the echo here is insane. "Like our voices could go on forever."

"They could."

The friends gulped.

"What're you doing here?"

Corey whirled around to face the old man. His wrinkled face was so close to his own.

"How did you get in here?"

"Oh, we um—" Corey looked down at the floor.

"You two come with me," the old man said. Grabbing the boys and taking them down a long hallway to a single room with a desk. It had a black notebook sitting upon it with a pen.

"How did you two get in?" The man asked.

The boys only stared at him. Corey didn't want to get in trouble, his gut was telling him to tell the truth, but what was he going to do? This man had to be crazy right? Living out here all alone for so long. Maybe he wouldn't get them in trouble.

"Uhh," the man grumbled. "How about this? I am Jack, the caretaker of this place. I used to live here when I was a kid, and I never left. Even after the kids did, to go to a better orphanage, out Roanoke way."

"Why not leave?" Billy asked not looking the man in the eye.

"How could I... It's the only home I have ever known. Would you leave on your own so easily?"

Jack had a point. Corey would definitely rather stay at his mom's than go anywhere else.

"How did y'all get in?" Jack asked again, his green eyes flickering.

"Um..." Corey couldn't bring himself to tell.

"What're your names, I'm calling the cops."

Corey didn't see a phone, so he wondered if the man was bluffing.

"Come on, tell me?"

"You mean three," Billy said.

Corey glanced to his side and only saw Billy. *Where is Cliff?*

"Where's Cliff?" Billy asked.

"What do you mean?" Jack asked, his face dropping.

"There were three of us. We ran through your basement to get up here. Sorry, we may've broken your door.

Jack jumped to his feet.

"No... No." The man ran out of the room. The boys followed. When they got back to the entrance corridor the door was open, and blood and viscera covered everything. *Cliff—no it couldn't be.*

Arms, fingers, and toes were thrown about the room. Corey held back a scream. Cliff, not Cliff.

Jack stood above something in the distance. A darkened spot just in front of the wide-open door.

Billy screamed and continued to scream for what felt like an eternity.

Corey found himself next to Jack. Cliff's head sat at his feet, pulsing blood across the tile floor. It filled every crevasse, every line, creating a mosque of grotesque gore.

Those dead blue eyes stared up at him. *What happened? And when?*

In one swift moment the old man reared back and stomped Cliff's head, skull fragments and brain blasting across the floor.

"What have you done?" Jack whispered. "What have *you* done?" Jack kicked what was left of Cliff's broken skull. "I have kept it at bay for so long." He turned and grabbed Corey. "Why would you do this?"

"I tried to stop—"

"I guess not good enough." The old man's grip was strong but not strong enough.

Corey pulled himself away, crashing to the floor.

"You have no idea what you've unleashed." The man fell to his knees. "We're all dead…" He muttered more under his breath that Corey couldn't make out. Then a silence fell across the room. Billy had stopped screaming.

Corey turned around and saw Billy, still standing in the same place staring at Corey. Something moved in the darkness behind him.

"Bill—"

A monster came out of the darkness. It was a giant spider with the mouth of a man. It grinned a grotesque grin, bigger than he had ever seen, right before it bit down on Billy, splitting his body in half. The spider shook its head twice before tossing the body in their direction.

It landed with a horrible splat on the floor and slid until it gently propped against Corey's foot. The blood shot out of Billy like one of those slasher films, only real. It splattered everywhere, and Billy gurgled before reaching out a hand.

Oh God he's still alive. He looked up at Corey, tears in his eyes.

"Help!" Billy gasped, before vomiting blood everywhere.

Corey tried to hold back the vomit, but it came crashing out, mixing with the blood that covered the floor.

Something landed gently in front of him, and bones crunched. Corey looked up into the huge red eyes of the monster, and it laughed. It stared down at him with evil filling its eyes. Corey's bladder let go.

Movement caught his eye. Something slammed into the spider thing before taking off down the hall.

Jack.

The monster screamed and ran after him, skittling on all eight legs. The echoes were almost overwhelming, ... Cliff... Billy... Oh God, everything Billy was still at his feet.

Corey forced himself to look down. Billy no longer moved, he was completely broken. Tears filled Corey's eyes as he stood.

I've got to help Jack.

Corey ran down the hall, and a roar echoed through the darkness. The monster was standing outside of the office. Jack must've gotten the door shut. He was safe.

Corey could leave and get help. The spider monster never looked at him, it just scratched on the door, trying to find its way in. Corey turned and ran; he had to get out the front door. A crash echoed behind him, followed by a rumble. The floor shook below him, and he almost fell to the ground. Stones bounced out of the ceiling. He dodged the first few, then something slammed into him, and stars burst before his eyes.

Corey couldn't get up, instead he rolled over. The stones came out one by one, falling all around him. The last thing he heard was a scream.

Corey's eyes opened. Pain raced through his entire body. Every breath hurt, he was on his back, the moon staring down on him. Corey smiled through the pain. A cough forced its way up, from deep within him, he tossed a hand up and blood filled his palm.

Oh God.

Corey tried to move but couldn't look down. His legs were crushed. He screamed into the night, and another scream answered him back. Corey laid his head back and looked toward the woods. In the distance was the spider. It gave one last scream and was one into the woods.

"Dammit," John said, as the blood hologram disappeared. He didn't need to see anymore; he knew what happened next. But that spider—he had never seen anything like it. Not in all his years working with the supernatural. It was almost as unsettling as the entity that stalked him.

John smiled. Okay, the plan had to be to kill the thing. Somehow Jack had at least knocked it off balance, that might mean his gun could work. He touched the holster.

John's gun was a gun like no other. It took the biggest bullet any revolver could take. It also had ten shots rather than the standard six. The thing was a monster of a gun. He pulled it out of his belt and opened it.

John never kept it loaded. God knew that ammo could kill someone easy, like super easy. *Got to love the government and their advanced tech.* Granted, it was needed if you wanted to take down a creature of the sort he was hunting now. Each bullet was about the size of his middle finger. He was the only one who could shoot the gun. Because of his *special condition* as Jasmine put it. God, he wished he could've kept the truth about him away from the others. But, oh well.

John slid the last bullet home. *I'm ready now.* He took in the woods around him where he hoped the monster wouldn't be waiting. "First time after a spider," John muttered. He needed to follow the path that the monster obviously made. John was lucky that the monster didn't head the other direction, it would've been a disaster. Too many people lived around Callaway, and he didn't need any more deaths.

The trees were parted in front of him, heading up the mountain. "Dammit." John walked forward, and to his right he saw it. The darkness was seeping through everything, the tentacles were appearing, taunting him. "Nope," he said, and continued up the path in front of him. *I can't deal with him right now.* Eventually he would need to, but today wasn't the day.

John kept his gun at the ready as he moved up the ridge. The underbrush crunched under his feet. The farther he went the more was damaged. The spider seemed to be just running. Not taking the time to really see where it was going. *If it can see.* The boys never saw if it had eyes. A sadness filled him. If only the boys stayed away, maybe Jack could've kept the thing at bay and the agency would've never picked up the readings that led him here. He would've stayed where he was, having a cold beer and waiting to hear from Silas. It was one of his favorite jobs, if he was being honest. Even if Silas did go rouge in his search for that bastard Simon King. It didn't mean anything, he was the backup for if Silas needed someone in whatever small town he had ended up in.

A squishing sound pulled him from his musings, and when he went to lift his boot, it was as if it was heavier than it was before. John glanced down to see a pile of web covering his boot.

"Gross," he said as he yanked his boot out of the substance. That stuff could be a problem. Ahead of him was a huge amount of it. The web covered the ground and the trees. The spider must've been making a nest, that was the only explanation. If it wasn't, then damn, he was going to have to stop it.

John had to overexaggerate his steps as he walked. Each one was like walking through spilled Coca Cola. The more he walked the crazier it got. The squishing sound was driving him crazy. There was no way he was going to escape this, nor give a sneak attack. *Fuck.*

It was going to know he was coming. Yet nothing moved ahead of him, he didn't even hear the birds chirping. Everything was silent. Which was not the norm in the mountains, you always heard something, especially in the summer. Sweat formed on his brow; damn it was a hot night.

John glanced at his watch. Four A.M. Two hours till sunrise. That spider was bigger than him so it could definitely outrun him. Unless…

Could it have been starving? Is that why it killed all of them? Was that Jack's plan all along?

Yes, that's the only thing that made sense.

A scream broke the silence in front of him, and John took off at a run.

The screaming was so loud, too loud. If this is what Jack had been living with then he couldn't blame him for being a bit odd and not being able to sleep. It was as if nails were being put through a meat grinder. At the crest of the ridge he was brought to a stop, almost sliding in the webbing. The clearing was a small one, in front of him the spider stood, he could only see its back in the pale moonlight.

Black fur like a tarantula's lined its back. The stiff hair reflected the light just so, and he could take in each strain individually. It was facing away from him. The whole area was filled with a thick webbing. In front of it was a deer gently kicking against its attacker. Blood dyeing the silky strands beneath it. Despite being a spider, it ate like a damn coyote

John slowly moved his way, trying his best not to alarm it with the jostling of the silk. His hand cannon stuck out in front of him. John only needed to get close enough to make sure that he was going to kill it in one shot. Deep inside he knew that even he might not be able to escape the thing. Even if he can't get hurt.

Squish.

Squish.

Only a little closer.

When he was ten feet away, he stopped and took aim. A smile crossed his face. John thought the mission would be way harder than it was turning out to be. John depressed the trigger, and the shot was deafening.

It would've been perfect too, but the dang thing jumped to the side just in time. John's bullet slammed into its rear leg, shooting it off into the distance in a spew of milky white blood. The monster screamed so loud that John had to cover his ears and, in an instant, it was charging at him, its bright white teeth gleaming in the low light. No eyes, no nothing.

It was so fast John was barely able to jump out of the way, rolling through the threads around him. It covered him head to toe in those damn strings. John forced himself to his feet, attempting to raise the gun, but it was already upon him again. He had no choice but to run. The ridge ended with a steep cliff that fell down into Franklin County. John slid as he tried to stop and almost fell. John barely stopped at the edge of the cliffside. Down below was maybe a two-hundred-foot drop into more trees. *There are too many damn trees here.* He smiled and spun on his heel.

"What do you want? Why do all this?" John called out.

The spider stopped in its tracks and tilted its head. "Freedom," it said in a deep, almost guttural voice. "Freedom taken from me for too long."

"Well, we can do that, but how do I know you aren't going to kill more."

"I must feed," it said, clicking its teeth.

Something moved in the darkness behind the spider. John smiled again. Lord was this thing in for a surprise.

"Well didn't you just finish lunch?" John asked, pointing toward the dead deer before remembering that it didn't have eyes.

"Not enough!" it roared.

The dark shape was almost upon the spider.

John raised his gun. "Well, you ain't eating me."

The spider charged and John fired two shots, both hitting it dead center. The scream it let out was haunting, people for miles had to have been able to hear it. A hole opened up in the gut of the monster, white blood splashing everywhere. The force of the blast propelled John backward into the air above that two-hundred-foot drop. He smiled as he fell. Another job well done. The last thing he saw was the spider being wrapped in that black tentacle, before disintegrating into nothingness.

John bounced when he hit the ground. *Fuck.* He lay motionless on the ground. It was never easy. He might not be dead, but he felt everything, and it took a moment for his bones to stick back together like they always do. But Mr. "*I want you back,*" at least finished off the monster.

After some time John stood, dusting himself off. *It wouldn't be a solo mission without me on the ground.* He cracked his neck and looked around the woods. "Where am I?" He muttered. A smile crossed his face. Time to walk till he found a road, so he put one foot in front of the other, and something dropped out of his coat.

John stared at it on the ground. The journal, he hadn't finished it. He picked it up and turned to the last entry.

July 22nd, 1990 Final Entry

I'm sorry. I fucking tried. I tried. My goal was to keep this secret. To make it up to Alice and Michael. Its screams became too loud.

Too much. If only those kids didn't come. It may have gone to the grave with me and died there, but it has starved for sixty years. How long does it take for it to finally die?

I locked myself in my room. But it's coming. It got through the door. Those damn kids.

My heart can't take this.

It's right outside the door. It will be here in no time. Nothing can hold it but that basement.

I don't know why that is. Some kind of magic.

Something that thing can't touch.

I hope someone finds this notebook. Find a way to stop it.

It's breaking through.

The man's pen slid down the page as if he died writing it.

He was an idiot. John closed the book and pocketed it for evidence; the director would want to see something. John walked deeper into the woods.

"The poor bastard."

Slipping Through the Veil

Death is unyielding, endlessly coming to the forefront. There is no running, no stopping, when it decides to come for you.

When I died, I wasn't scared, I wasn't alone, I wasn't anything. It was my duty and I protected her first and foremost. She was terrified the shooter was en route. Being the president's daughter made it harder, especially when times were as dire as they were.

Politically, everything was shit. People were throwing jabs at each other left and right, fights in the streets, people were dying. Yet none of it was reported. None of it verified. Hell, the shooter wasn't even a given, but we did have a threat. Thus, the president wanted her to stay in her apartment and never leave. The girl was independent and didn't want her father's political leanings to dictate her life.

She was going to be a regular twenty-year-old, no matter what her father said. So, we went to the mall. Marie was everything to me. Not just because I was the lead of her security, but because she was a beautiful person. A ray of sunshine in every single way, but her father was way too overbearing. He insisted that every available agent be with his daughter at all times.

The day after the threats began, my Superior took me to the side, since I was the youngest member of the detail, as well as having the most supervision experience due to my time in the army. "Agent Nelson, you need to be on your "A" game. The president wants ten men with Marie at all times." I nodded.

"Okay, sir." And that was that. I didn't ask questions, I didn't say no, I followed orders. But she didn't want an army following her.

"Please, John," she whispered as she caressed my cheek. "Can't we go to the mall? It could be our first date."

I smiled. Yes, it was wrong to be in a relationship with the president's daughter, but I couldn't say no. We were in love. Complete and total love. It didn't start that way, it just kind of happened. Thinking back to it, a smile always crosses my face. Her radiant smile, the memory of her bright blonde hair always comes back. Her hazel eyes, digging into me, not knowing the tragedy that would befall us based on my decision. My one damn decision. No, it was more than one.

We had slept together within a week of knowing each other, we were...she had just...no, I can't say it. Not with me dying and everything.

I sighed. "Okay, but the others."

"Can't you get them away."

I gripped her hand in mine. "Of course." As I left the room I couldn't help but smile and finger the box in my pocket. A ring. One just for her. We hadn't known each other long, but I knew she was the one. Was it stupid? Probably. Was it too soon? Definitely, but that didn't matter to me as I made my way to the HQ of the apartment building. We had set it up in the basement to keep an eye on everything. It is where the other guys would be at this hour. "Lunch time," I whispered.

I was sure of my plan almost immediately. It had only two steps to it. Tell the others that the president needed them and run the fuck out the door to my car.

From there I would drive us to the mall, where it would be just the two of us. To this day I don't know if her father found out about us, but I guess it doesn't matter now. I just wish I could still feel her warmth. The beautiful energy that lit up every room, but that wasn't meant for us. Maybe we were never meant to be.

As I entered the room where the others were, they all looked up. I tried to put on my most serious face as I busted through the door.

"What's wrong John?" One of them asked. He was a tall guy with pasty skin, his suit was too tight, and it ruined the secret service look.

"President needs you, suspected shooter at the White House," I screamed, doing my best to emulate the drill sergeants I had dealt with in the Army.

They all jumped to their feet.

"What about Ms. Kiser?" The same kid asked.

"I'll handle them, you just Go, Go, Go!"

Without a second thought, they all left the room. From inside I could hear their vehicles start and zoom away. I smiled and felt a gentle touch on my back. I whirled around, and Marie was on me. Kissing like we had never kissed before.

When she finally pulled away, she whispered. "Let's go."

I got us to the mall around 1 P.M. "Remember," I began as I put the vehicle in park. "We have maybe an hour or two before anyone notices we are gone."

"Let's go then," Marie said, and giggled as she jumped out of the car.

I had to run just to catch her, "Marie, stop."

"John, this isn't a workday, it's a date." She pecked my cheek.

I could tell I was reddening. *We're out in public, what is she doing?*

The mall that day was a blur of me following her around everywhere. There was chatter on my radio, but I ignored it. I knew there would be hell to pay, but the time with Marie was so much more important. We held hands gently as we ate Chick Fil A, then we went to every dress shop she could find. As I watched her, my love grew stronger. She was the one. I would do anything for her, even quit my job to be with her.

We got ice cream and turned around to find a young man talking with her.

"Come on girl, give me your digits," the kid said in a pretend hip voice.

"I told you no,"

"Nobody tells me no, yo. You're hot as hell."

Marie glanced over his shoulder, spotting me, and smiled.

"See I told you." He reached out a hand quick as lightning and grabbed her breast. "Come with me and I'll show you a good time."

"Leave her be," I said with as much authority as I could muster.

The kid spun around. I had seen the type a million times, flat bill cap pulled over dark eyes, pimply face, and a band t-shirt. The kid was a tool and could do nothing but cause women trouble at every turn. Always looking for that next fuck.

"Who the fuck do you think you are?" He asked, but I think the suit spooked him.

"You know who she is?" I asked, as I gave her the ice cream.

Marie gave a gentle smile. "Thank you, John."

The boy swung at me in an instant. Kids who think they are hot shit tend to do such things. Sadly, for him, I was too good for him to fuck with.

I grabbed his hand and spun it around. He flipped through the air and slammed onto the tile floor. His breath shot out of him as he screamed. I gave him one quick kick to the face, and he was out.

The ice cream shop went silent, everyone in shock, a few looked as if they were going to call the cops.

"Secret service, sorry you had to witness this. If someone could get an authority to take him away, the country and President would appreciate it."

With that I sat and ate the ice cream. Halfway through, Marie grabbed my hand and mouthed a *thank you*. I gave her a nod in return. Then it was back to the shops.

Everything was going great until the silence caught my attention. We were in the middle of the mall, and it should've been loud for hours yet. I glanced at my watch, 4 P.M. Nowhere close to closing time. I glanced around while Marie continued walking. A man stood on the balcony above us. Without a second thought I ran. *I got to make it.* I slammed into Marie, knocking her to the ground, just as a shot echoed out. A hot searing pain entered my torso just above my navel and exited through my upper back. The pain was unbearable, but it was followed by a coldness I didn't understand as my heart pumped out more of my blood through the wounds.

The police showed up quickly. I guess it was because no one else was shot but me. I found out later that I was the target, not Marie for whatever reason.

Marie was on her knees above me with my blood covering her hands. She held the spot in my stomach. She yelled but I couldn't make out what was said. The ice slipped over me like a blanket. The world became dark, well, kind of fuzzy at the edges. Tears ran down my cheek. The last thing my eyes saw were her hazel eyes. In that moment, my heart broke, I lost something I would never get back, and I...

I died.

I know that for certain. Despite reading this seeming to confirm something different because if I died how could I write this all out. Well, there is something beyond, like they all say, but it ain't a bright light or a beautiful gate. It's nothingness. Complete and total nothingness. Fuck, I hope I never go back.

I opened my eyes in an immense darkness. I could tell I was moving fast, I tried to speak, to move, to do anything, but couldn't. *What the hell?* An abyss opened up in front of me and at the center of it was a moving mass of something I couldn't make out. Colors popped within, faces appeared and disintegrated. They screamed and writhed under thin shiny skin.

No, they weren't faces but skulls.

I imagine I would have screamed if I had my mouth, but I didn't.

My chest jutted. Pain, or a facsimile of pain, filled my soul.

Where is God? Where is the devil? My mind wasn't comprehending what was being shown to me. Could all the religions of the world really be wrong?

The darkened mass surrounded me. Eyes protruded from a stomach like an appendage, and arms sprang to life and pointed at me.

The voices sang "*help us*" before disintegrating into a deep laughter. A mouth opened in the stomach of the thing.

It spoke in what I thought was a bastardized Latin.

It smiled, teeth gleaming red in the blackness. Its eyes shone a blue that was intoxicating. I moved toward it against my will as it laughed. I realized that this is where all souls go. This was the one and only place. The afterlife was in the belly of this monster that floated in the blackness.

My chest pinged again, as if some feeling was returning to my broken body. I was almost to those horrible teeth when a hand materialized above me. It grabbed me and pulled me into the air. Its fingers were the color of sunrise as it shimmered.

My eyes opened, and I gasped for air. I was on a table surrounded by candles, which sat at the apex of each point of a pentagram. *What the hell is going on?*

"It worked," said a voice. I turned my dead eyes toward the sound. My sight was blurry and my ears were muffled.

"Who's there?" I tried to say, but a ghastly moan came out instead. Then she was upon me. My Marie.

"You're back," she said. My stiff neck creaked as I nodded. I was unsure of what had just happened, but happy I had returned to her.

"Can you not talk?"

A moan escaped me again; she smiled and kissed my cold lips. Her warmth was intoxicating. Her eyes filled with fear.

"The book said you would be well again."

I am. I tried to say to no avail. *I am alive.*

"Did I wait too long?"

I shook my head in one slow motion. *Dammit, why can't I speak.* I reached out a hand to her. It happened in slow motion.

"Good, good."

I looked down. I was naked, with a hole of torn flesh just above my navel. There was no sensation in me, no warmth, no heartbeat. *What.* I tried to sit up and she helped me.

"I love you; we can be together now. Especially since they think you are dead. No one will ever know," Marie said with a broken smile. Tears swam across her cheeks.

" I love you too," I croaked. It took me a long time, but I could do it. I was sure in time it would get better. I shook my arms in an attempt to get rid of the stiffness and slung one of them around her, hugging her close to me.

She smiled, her eyes the deepest blue. *But weren't they hazel before?*

A scream echoed all around me and darkness streamed out of the floor, filling the air like smoke. Hands broke out of the ground. Marie screamed as the hands grabbed her. In an instant she was sucked into the darkness, merging with the others. Her body danced within as she disintegrated, leaving a bobbing, screaming skull beneath the dark skin.

The eyes appeared first, filling me with fear. The mouth appeared next and bit down on what was left of Marie, and blood splattered across me.

The monster smiled at me. Evil unyielding, and it spoke.

"A soul for a soul. I watch. Forever watch."

It held me in its gaze. Marie saved me at the cost of her own life. Part of me wishes I was still dead. As it shrunk away, a tentacle shot out, and my skin seared. "Marked you are. You must always run." As the monster disappeared a fear filled me. I will never forget that translucent ever-changing face.

I looked down at my wrist, where the skin still bubbled. A skull spanned most of the wrist's width, its mouth wide open as if in a scream. The word *run* written within the open mouth. The fear welled up within me again, and I stood on shaky legs and ran.

Running is all I have done since. At first, each step was as if I was made of wax. My body was hard and rigid. It took days for me to get back to feeling like myself. Later, I realized how long I had been dead. Almost a week. I also found out that Marie had exhumed my body to do the ritual.

She is considered missing now, but what the hell can I do? I am dead to the whole world but. . .the darkness still chases me. Luckily, I was able to keep my name, but I can never speak about my former life. Hence, why I am writing it down here. How it began... and how I fell apart.

In the wake of Marie being taken, she haunted my thoughts, my world, my everything. I loved her, and she brought me back, just to die as well. She would've haunted my dreams if I could sleep, but I can't. When I run, I don't feel the pump of my heart. My temp adjusts to the weather around me. Everything is awful. Sometimes I wonder if I should've fucking gone into the beast, been consumed. At times I wonder if I should let it catch me, but a fear always fills me at the thought of becoming one with that thing.

It is always there though. I can never completely stop moving, as it sits at the edge of my vision. Just beyond where I think is safe. *Can someone help me?* I wasn't sure as I walked down the street. I was now far from Washington D.C. A road sign appeared from the dark. *Welcome to Roanoke County.* I sighed. I should've gone North, closer to New York, to home, but I couldn't do it because I was considered dead. I wasn't going to show up on my mother's stoop, just for her to fall apart. Fuck, she might even die from the shock.

I slunk down next to the sign. *I could just let him take me. End this all.* In that moment of weakness, I was ready to die. To fall away from everything, but at the same time in the back of my mind, I remembered Marie's sacrifice. Within that beast, she wouldn't want me to stay this way. She brought me back for a reason.

A wind shuddered through the surrounding woods. If I could still feel I would've shivered, but I felt nothing. It was as if I was a vampire, but worse. In the distance something fluttered, it slammed into my face. I pulled it away as quickly as I could. A newspaper, it was turned halfway through the paper itself. In the dim light of the moon shone down upon a single article. "Need help? Call me today, for all magical arts." I took it as odd, but what was I going to do? At this point it seemed like a sign from God. Even if I didn't believe in Him anymore. I stood and walked into the dark, for what felt like forever. There was no address on the paper, but as I walked, I turned without thinking. I walked through the woods, I crossed roads, all against my volition. It was as if I was being led where I needed to go.

Days and nights came; in time I wondered if I would simply walk forever. Finally, a house came into view, a small cabin shrouded in woods, sunflowers lining the sides of the porch. Upon the porch sat a single woman, rocking in a chair.

"The winds have brought you, cold one," she said in a raspy voice. "But you ain't a blood sucker. You seem to be something else."

I don't know what compelled me, but I showed her my right wrist, and the mark that scarred it. She didn't flinch.

"Ah, Death's mark, you were saved, huh? Doesn't happen often you know." She rubbed her gnarled finger across the place the mark sat. "The energy is unbelievable."

She pulled back her hood, revealing herself fully for the first time. White hair danced down to her shoulders, her face was deeply lined, yet her almost grey eyes dug into me. As if they were trying to remove every part of who I am... of who I was.

"You died, but the cost to live was greater. A girl, me thinks," she said standing to her full height, which was barely to my shoulder.

"How can you—"

"Come child, it's my gift. I can help you find a way to sever your ties. Or . . ."

She stared at me with those light eyes,

"Or...what?"

"You can harness the power."

Hilda was like no other person I had ever met. Adept in what we would call magic. Which was something I didn't think was real for most of my life. However, she could do it all, scrying, crystal ball, even blood magic. Which seemed to be what I was most adept in. I stayed with her through the summer of 1990, and it was the best time of my life.

I learned more than I could have thought about the realm beyond. My connection to that realm is what made me a natural. Yet I also learned of so much beyond ourselves in that time. But I was determined in the end to learn as much as I could, even if it scared me, and it fucking did.

"Take your time son, there is no hurry," Hilda whispered after I told her my plan. "I know you're angry, but it will not help you. However, I just need you to do one thing. Look into the ball, it will show you what you wish. Then make your decision."

I begrudgingly agreed, the globe was one of those typical ones that the fake Magik practitioners used. I knew this wasn't the case with Hilda. She was true in every way. I mean, shit, she brought warmth back to my skin, when it shouldn't have been possible. No blood pumped through my veins. I literally had a hole through my abdomen that had barely healed over. Yet she did it.

The clouds danced deep within the ball before parting. I could see Marie and I walking, then a figure appeared on the balcony behind me. Shrouded in darkness, I could not make out the face. Anger flared within me. I wanted to know who it was. How had they done what they had? Where did they come from?

"Calm yourself, dead one," Hilda whispered, placing a hand on my shoulder.

I took a breath. "I know what I must do."

"Then be on with it."

I thanked her and left the house. As I passed the threshold of the door there was a soft pop, and I turned around. The house was gone, a sunflower field stood where it was.

I sighed and kept walking. *I should've known.*

Revenge paves the road to death, Hilda's voice whispered through the wind. I wish I had listened.

The mall was exactly how I remembered it. It didn't take me long to find the spot; I even thought that I may have spotted a little of my blood stuck in between the tiles. My eyes glanced up to the balcony where the shooter would've been. I whispered to myself in the old tongue that Hilda had taught me. Taking a deep breath, my eyes danced across the mall as if on their own. Slipping around until they landed on a balcony two floors above.

A shadowy shape flickered in and out of existence. When I blinked, it was gone. I wandered up and down the steps till I found the spot. As I stood there I focused on my needs. The shadow reappeared and took a vague shape. Glasses came into view, a single man that I recognized. If my heart was still beating it would've dropped. My boss stared down where I stood. A smile plastered across his face. "What the fuck Perkins?" Why had he killed me? Why? Why would he betray his country in such a way? It made no sense to me.

A rage rose up from deep within me. My heart threatened to burst back to life. Unlucky for him, I knew where he would be.

I turned, and a black tentacle slashed for me. Instinctively I jumped off the balcony. *How did I let it so close?*

Someone screamed below, I felt a soft crunch when I hit, but nothing more.

"Call 911!" someone yelled. "Wait, don't move your—" She didn't finish as I ran for my life. Inside me it was as if the bones were healing, things creaked and popped back into place. Before I knew it, I could run again with a hobble.

People screamed behind me, but I gave them no mind. Later the news would say it was a miracle. But really, it's a curse. Either way, I had only one thing on my mind. Killing Perkins.

I approached my former place of work with caution. The black suit and pale complexion helped me blend in. Luckily, I found some sunglasses as well so that no one could see my sunken eyes. If they did, the shock would prove that I was nothing but a corpse.

I pushed through the door, and no one asked a single question. Simply acting as though you belong goes a long way.

I turned down the hallway toward where Perkins would be. Even though I didn't have any weapons, I was sure that I could end him. It would be the simplest thing I have ever done.

I smiled as I went to knock on the door.

"Agent, what're you doing?" A voice shouted from behind me.

"I needed to talk to the chief." I turned. A small man stood not too far from me, his own suit way too big.

"He isn't here. Remember, the President's big speech is tonight. Perkins is watching over everything."

I took a step forward. "Where's the speech again?"

"Lincoln memorial, how could you forget?"

"Brain fart, I guess," I said as I ran for the exit. Once again, no questions were asked. But one thing I knew. Perkins would die.

The light was starting to dissipate as I arrived. I smiled, ready for it. Marie would get her revenge. *Perkins, you son of a bitch.*

I watched from my spot in the crowd. The President had just come on to give his speech, but I didn't give a damn. I pushed my way through the crowd until I could see Perkins to the President's left, but something wasn't right, he had his gun drawn.

"No, no," I screamed and jumped on stage, ready to kill.

People screamed as I slammed into Perkins. A shot went off and slipped through the flesh and bone of my shoulder.

"Who the fuck," Perkins slammed a fist into my head knocking, my glasses off my face. "John."

He recognized me and was completely taken aback. Perkins aimed the gun again and I didn't flinch. The bullet entered my forehead, my brain matter splattered against the crowd, and yet I kept going. There was no way he was getting away.

Fear filled his eyes, as surprise crossed his face and he aimed the gun again, but this time his hand shook.

I knocked it away. "Why?" I asked. "You were the perfect soldier. I thought we were friends."

He spit in my face. "Like we could be friends after what you did, taking her from me."

My hand slipped around his throat. "You loved her?"

"No, but the Damned needed her." He laughed as a gunshot rang out. I looked over in time to see the bullet pass through the President's head. He crashed to the ground. Everyone screamed. I looked back at Perkins, he smiled. "He will return."

I squeezed his neck with a power I didn't know I had. There was a loud crunch, and he fell limp.

I stood, my body shaking. I looked between the bodies, and as I watched, a mist lifted out of each of them. Followed by those black tendrils I have come to know.

Each of them grabbed and pulled the mist into the unending darkness below our realm.

I stood to run; it was too close for comfort. However, a bullet slammed into my knee and I collapsed.

"Police, don't move!" I did as they said. They handcuffed me, but when they looked at my face, they had to push their gaze away.

The hole in my head must've been too much for them.

Then I was in the car, then off to the station, where I was fingerprinted, then led into a separate room.

The interrogation room was one of the worst. I had been in here for what felt like years. When they asked my name, I would only tell them John. In the mirror-like window I could see the wound had healed some. It was like my body was going back to its initial dead state. I sighed.

At least I got through things, but who were the Damned? Why did they do any of this?

My mind couldn't wrap around any of it.

The door opened and I looked up. A man I hadn't seen before stood in the doorway. His black hair was slicked back from his face. His piercing blue eyes stared into me. The man's dress caught me off guard; he was wearing a damn flannel. "Killed the President huh?"

"No." I stopped. This ass wasn't going to listen to me.

The man smiled as he pulled something out of his pocket and clicked it. A surge of sound whirled around us and the man ran forward.

"We don't have much time." He smiled. "The Damned did this, didn't they?"

I nodded.

He smiled. You want to help finish them." He held out a hand.

I took it. "Of course,"

"Well, welcome to the ranks." He twirled his hand as if wanting me to say something.

"John."

"Nice to meet you, I'm Silas, and you're in for a hell of an adventure."

The Blue Mist

"We got to get out of 'ere, before that sombitch comes back," Allan said as he slammed the door to the old homeplace.

"What was that, unc?" Jack asked.

"I ain't got no clue, but we're safe 'ere."

What was that? That thing in the hunting shed. It wasn't no bear...

He knew that if it was a bear, there was no stopping it from coming through the damned door. The door made an awful cracking sound as the wind pummeled it.

"Where did the fog come from?" Jack asked.

For a boy of thirteen, he is taking this whole situation well.

Allan looked out the window into the blue mist. The wind howled as the hail beat against the tin roof.

"I ain't sure, but it ain't natural. Now get on to the kitchen and see if you can find a light. This building hasn't got power." He heard Jack walk away toward the old kitchen while he watched the mist.

Allan saw shapes move within the blue. Allan's heart ran like a steam train in his chest. His breath shot in front of him. It almost crystallized in front of him.

Part of him wondered if it would drop to the floor and shatter. That's how cold it was.

We should've never hunted in this storm.

The hairs on the back of his neck stood up.

Are we safe here?

Allan glanced around the old house. It was his father's, father's, father's. He is in the living room just past the entryway, the old carpet is coated with frost from one side of the room to the other. Some animals had ripped the carpet to shreds, but that's to be expected from a long-abandoned house. The color of the carpet had changed to a dark black, compared to the original milky brown.

The walls were all-natural wood paneling from a time before his. He could see it peeling, a clear sign of water damage which also discolored it to a disgusting yellow hue. It broke his heart to see the state of the house, but it wasn't time to think about that. Above him, he could see the holes in the tin roof where little flakes of hail fell through before bouncing off the carpet. The blue mist seemed to almost be invading the house as Allan watched it seep through the hole.

"You okay, Jack?" Allan called, but he received no answer. He made his way toward the kitchen and heard the slight crack of the frost under his boots. Walking through that house was like walking into a fun house. The floor sloped downward as he approached the kitchen, where the tile sloped at an even steeper angle. He was looking at the old cabinets; all half fallen, when he heard a scream behind him.

Before he knew it, his feet were in the air, and he slammed hard into the tile before sliding down the slope into the old cabinet. He barely held on to his rifle. The cabinets crunched under his weight. Pain filled his body as he tried to right himself.

He looked back toward the front door and saw nothing but baby blue mist, and then a figure. The figure was tall and wore black clothes, almost like a trench coat. The thing was bulky, almost like a bear. Its face was a horrible conglomeration of different animals. It had a long snout, like a bear, with two sharp black incisors that stood out from the rest of its teeth. The sight of the thing's smile was like an icepick to Allan's heart. Above its nose, it had the ears of a wolf and no eyes. Where there should've been eyes was only slick black skin. The thing raised its right claw-like hand, and the skin split apart, revealing a single purple eye. One that sent terror through Allan's body.

What the hell?

He aimed his rifle without thinking and took a single shot at the creature. The sound echoed through the house. The thing shrunk as it fell to the ground.

Jack's body slid to him down the slope, and blood ran down toward him. It soaked him. Allan stared in horror at his nephew. He looked up and saw the thing had returned. It raised one finger to its snout in a shhh gesture and disappeared into the mist. Allan screamed into the surrounding mist, clutching Jack as the mist closed in around him.

The Truth Within

November 24th, 1972

What had gone wrong? What the fuck had gone wrong? He had done every-thing right. Everything, yet he still ended up here. He still failed. It made no sense. He'd said the incantations and completed sacrifices. The only thing he missed was the Sword boy dying.

Simon ran his hand through his hair. What could he have done though? He followed his grandfather's book to a T. What was needed was the Sword boy. Why hadn't he just shot him instead of Cecil. It would've made things so much fucking easier. He had the chance and even lined up the shot as the boys dug. All he had to do was switch the gun from Cecil to Silas, and he would've won. The final sacrifice would've been made, and his life could've continued. But what if the beast had to consume him? That's why. The last sacrifice wouldn't have worked if he wasn't alive.

Fuck, but he didn't know that, how could he have ruined the plan? It was so many years in the making. His grandfather had killed Jeremiah just for this. The perfect sacrifice, but he still ruined almost sixty years of preparation. Even the lynching of the Jackson woman was leading toward this moment.

She was in the way, and he wasn't going to let the old witch stop the plan. The fire danced in his mind. *God, was it good, it was right!* Just as the King in Yellow would want.

He stood from the bed looking down at his hand, where the symbol glowed. A soft golden shine, if only he had the courage to push the knife in sooner. *Maybe you would've succeeded.* A voice said in his head. *Maybe he would be free, and she would be revived.*

"Maybe so," Simon whispered.

Then do something about it. A chill ran through Simon, and his heart ran like a stallion. Nothing had ever spoken back to him before. *Simon, we are closer than ever.*

I must be going mad. Simon had been racking his brain for so long it had become hard to focus, and now he was hearing voices. *What the fuck.* Food. That's what he needed, too bad the motel didn't have breakfast. If it did things would've been so much easier. Simon didn't want to go far from his room. Not while he figured it all out. So many people died... too many people and it was his fault. Granted, he didn't really care, but he had to figure out how to get the power his grandfather promised. To bring *her* back, but it seemed like that dream was not possible.

Either way, the realm beyond our own had opened up to him in a way he never expected. Maybe he needed to check the diary. Yes, that could help... there had to be something he missed. Some type of wisdom or somewhere else he could go, other rituals he could do, people he could interact with. Simon took in the room. It wasn't the best one, but he made do. Not that you can find much in the southwestern part of Virginia, along I-81. He was maybe fifty miles from where Three Forks used to be. Only fifty damn miles.

The room was 'clean' by motel standards. A single bed with scratchy sheets sat in the middle of the room. A grimy carpet that used to be some sort of puffy yellow shag danced across the floor. The mirror was smudged and the bathroom was downright small, just enough room for a bath and a toilet. But they were smashed together in some odd ass hodge podge manner, making it nearly impossible to use. It wasn't what he was used to as mayor, but it was something, and he only had the money he had stored in the truck, so beggars couldn't be choosers.

The plan had been so simple. Joe and him were going to cause some trouble. They would sacrifice the Sword family—But ole Maynard fought too hard. They killed them. In the process the two of them kind of went mad. The King in Yellow was all that fluttered in their minds, the symbol of his coming, yet either his grandfather had played quite a trick on him, or the ritual wasn't right. He had gotten no power, not even an ounce, and that was scary. These things from beyond were hard to deal with, and Simon's grandfather made it seem like a power would be granted to him. A power that would change him into something better, turn him into a fucking God, and he could bring Shelia back.

Yet he thought after he was forced to kill Joe that things would get better, that it would be easier, but it wasn't. Instead, they caused even more problems for him. Then he thought maybe killing Cecil would be enough, but that failed as well. Everything he ever did failed, and it broke his heart. It really did. *I should've killed Sword, instead of trusting he would get close enough.*

Yes, you should've. Said the mocking voice that had plagued his dreams since he was a kid. The voice that had changed everything and turned him into who he was. Ever since the day he found the damn notebook. Yet he wouldn't change it for the world. It promised him power, a power he would take sooner or later, and that's what scared him. *Power comes at a cost.*

Simon thought the cost would end up being the whole town of Three Forks. Yet the one person he needed to kill, was the one he failed to. Then the monsters went out of his control and almost killed him. Their slick faces haunted his dreams, consumed by the one all-knowing eye. Purple in a split hand. His grandfather hadn't specified anything about how they looked, just the notions.

Just that the horror writers of old weren't using their imaginations. They were connected to a realm of very real elder beings. Ones that even Lovecraft couldn't fully imagine, ones that wanted nothing more than to take their rightful place back in our world.

His mind floated away, back to the day he found it.

The notebook that would change his life.

Simon's heart slammed in his chest. To the point that he wasn't sure what would happen. He had never snuck into his father's study before. Growing up in Floyd County, Virginia, he wasn't privy to much. Even if his father was one of the richest people in the county, he never truly showed any type of love for his son, and Simon never knew where the wealth came from.

Simon wasn't sure why he made his way into the study. *Go.* A voice had said in his head. It had never been there before, but being only five years old he thought it was normal. *Your father hides stuff from you.* Really? Could his dad really be hiding stuff from him? Granted, he rarely ever saw him, but still... Come to think of it, he didn't know much about the King family. Nor his mother's. Simon's Daddy didn't like to talk about her, whenever he did a sadness would fill his deep blue eyes, and they would lose their light. Despite him being an incredibly well-liked man, there was always a sadness about him.

Simon tried to ignore the voice in his head, but he couldn't after the phone call he overheard.

"I told you not to call here again," a voice spoke on the other end that Simon couldn't hear. "My dad had beliefs, but I don't have a diary. I don't have it, now leave me. Never call again." His dad slammed the phone and stormed out of the room. "Damned fuckers."

Simon knew what he needed to do. Find that diary.

Inside, the study was sparse. There were bookshelves that lined the walls, but they were completely empty, with a desk that sat at the center.

Why was the room so empty? It made no sense to Simon. On the desk sat only a book. It was old, older than any book he had ever seen. It had to be lambskin.

He picked it up, and a chill ran through his body as he touched the soft skin. At that moment the book became his.

His father looked for it for years, but Simon hid it in a hole in the wall of his room. It wasn't till later that he realized how important it was. It led him to The King in Yellow; it led him to killing all those people. Sometimes he wondered what his younger self would think of him now.

He smiled. Simon truly didn't care what his younger self thought. He didn't give a flying fuck. The only thing that mattered was the diary. It was always the same process. When he felt lost, he would have an almost uncontrollable urge to revisit it. Now he was more lost than he had been in years and wanted to do everything he could to right what he got wrong, to connect to that other realm. Simon walked to the small desk where a backpack sat and pulled out the small black book.

The answers had to be somewhere, and he was going to find them. His heart sank at the thought of having to figure out the world again, but he needed to go on the journey one last time. Give me guidance. *Read.* The voice said, it hadn't spoken in so long. He really must've been having a hard time. His failures were going to kill him. In the most literal sense. All that death was on his hands. Was he really feeling guilty? No... He was—*read dammit.* The voice screamed, and he did.

June 18th, 1915: The Truth

I find myself broken to the point where everything that I had lain over the past forty years seems to have fallen into an abyss of my own making. My plans, despite careful planning, have become overbearing. They creak into the darkness of my soul, as if seeping through every pore, even as the cough becomes worse. Threatening everything I have done, everything I have created, everything I have seen. As my mind drifts back to the early days, I find myself having trouble holding my pen. My mind is fogging lately as I try to write. In my seventy years on this Earth, my mind has never felt so slow. As if a slug had seeped into my very heart, before slipping up into my brain. Stopping my thoughts from forming, stopping the world from moving, stopping me from articulating as fully as I want to. Thus, I have decided to write everything down, before my mind forgets what I have done, and I fall into an abyss from which I will never return.

My mind is my greatest asset, so alas, if I was to lose it, how much of myself would I lose as well. This dreadful tale of darkness would also be lost, and I cannot let my efforts fall to the wayside. If that were to happen it would all be for naught. I do sometimes wonder if it is the sickness or my advanced age that steals the clarity from my thoughts. Granted, I have met multiple people in my travels who lived into their nineties. They lived happy lives until they died in their bed, but I doubt I can receive the same peaceful death, as the pain wells up somewhere deep within my chest. That was what I always wanted for myself. A peaceful death, a return to my Elizabeth. Especially during the war, yet I know it isn't what awaits me. My fate has been sealed for quite some time. Ever since I started the path, since that battle, since we followed that strange man into the darkness of the woods.

I digress. Here I am, living in a world that is at war. The eve of the end seems to be coming, and I am unsure if my work will change anything or if anyone will read this. Others in the world know of the things I have touched. They also use the power, yet protecting this country will go beyond me, as I am too old to fight again. I await the invasion, and those who would bring America to its knees. Just as we almost did. I'm not one who fought for the union or the confederacy, I was fighting for my place in the world. Our militia might have existed within the confederacy, but our town of Three Forks fought for itself. Fought to stay out of the damn war. We attempted to fight off both sides during the war to protect our town.

We stood our ground, fighting for ourselves and our families, until we were pulled into the confederate army. We had no choice. They took the town, killed our mayor, and forced all the boys to fight since they had killed all the older men, leaving only us kids behind to deal with it. I was forced to bury my own father. I watched as they tortured and raped my mother and abused my brothers. The beating was something that only stopped when I agreed to join the army. Leaving behind my family, my town, my world... Lord help me for the things I was forced to do. Yet God does not sit with many anymore, he walked away on the ground in Gettysburg, if he ever existed at all. As I watched my fellow people die all around me. We didn't care for the politics of it all, and so many of the kids I fought with never got to see Three Forks again. The two of us that did return, came with a plan. With a power that was beyond our own. Our town would never be taken again. It was ours; we lived it, we worked it. *I was never going to let someone take our town again.* Even if Jeremiah got in the way.

I am rambling, and I apologize for that, there is just so much that needs to be said within these pages. Whoever reads this, I only ask that you use it as a way to continue my work. Please, because the power hidden within these words has the ability to change everything. To bring us out of the shadows, to make sure we are never forgotten again. The mountains are dark and deep and hide so many secrets. We are the forgotten ones. The ones who wait for dusk, the ones who remember a time before complete corruption. We are the ones who will destroy the bearcats that have taken advantage of us. The rich mine owners will not hold us under their thumbs any longer. We, like our forefathers, will take things into our own hands, but at a cost.

We are the Damned.

Whoever you are, I hope you see the truths I have found. Because the world needs change, and we will be the catalyst.

July 3rd,1863: Gettysburg, Pennsylvania

Orders were orders, I didn't like it, but I had no choice. We had been fighting for two long days, waiting for General Lee to truly get us to break through. The rumors around camp the night before reported that Lee had a plan that would get us through the union line and into Gettysburg proper. This, however, was not described to us till the next morning, as the tired men who didn't want to be in the damn state gathered around. The plan was to move with the force of twelve thousand men to attack. We were going to charge with Picket as our leader, our divisions were to be the right flank on the attack moving forward after the union artillery had mostly been destroyed.

We stood in line waiting side by side. It was an old form of warfare. Nothing like the warfare that is being seen today in Europe, no trenches, no bombs, the standards were very different then. The two armies usually faced each other and fired. The idea being to take out as many of the other troops as possible. I had to suppress myself from jumping as the cannons shot at each other across the ridge line. We were waiting for the firing on the union side to stop, showing that we had destroyed all of their artillery.

I stood stark still, my musket hefted up onto my shoulder, listening to the cannon fire and waiting for the dreaded order. Moving forward was something I didn't want to do, and being as I was forced to be part of the army, they were keeping a close eye on me. Henry, Levin, and the twins Jeremiah and Nehemiah stood side by side. Waiting.

We didn't usually talk in these lines. I had been at the front of many battles, but I had never stood for this long. The humidity of the day was wearing on me. The sun stood high in the sky telling me it may be past noon. We had been standing since six that morning, waiting for the order, yet it hadn't come. The firing didn't start till hours after we lined up. My body ached; it wasn't meant for standing this long. I don't think anyone's is. My heavy uniform had already soaked through, and it stuck to my skin, making me itchier than I can describe. My heart slammed in my chest, as if a little rabbit had taken up residence there.

"Fire," followed by the artillery was all I could hear, but between it, me and the other three boys would talk. They called us the three boys because of our hometown, even though there were actually five of us. Jeremiah and Nehemiah were always the odd one out in those counts, he was from one of the most prestigious families in Three Forks. His dad had been the mayor, and his uncle the town constable before the confederates killed them. He was never able to get over their deaths. Granted we all lost people then, I lost someone. Nehemiah on the other hand never really spoke. He just did as he was asked, never worrying about what anyone had to say.

"Do you think we'll die?" Levin asked. He stood right next to me. Three months' worth of beard lined his face, so I could barely see his beady brown eyes out of the hair. I had always wished I could grow a beard like his. I still haven't, even all these years later, but either way Levin was a good friend, even if he was a bit craven.

"It's possible. I reckon we won't get back to Virginia. We followed Lee a bit too far north," I said, as I quickly reached up a hand to wipe my brow. Each of us knew there was no "*following*" involved in what we did. We were forced to fight, or we would die like the others. Then Three Forks truly would've been a massacre. The boys and I didn't talk much about that though, we didn't need to reminisce on our confinement. Shit, it was all too obvious from our placement. Front of the line, where we would be the first to die.

"Don't speak of the General in that manner. We don't know who may be listening," Henry said. He continued to stare forward, watching the cannonballs slam into the positions of the Union artillery. Luckily, it seemed like our side was getting louder while the enemy was getting softer.

"The general can kiss—" I began.

"Stop it!" Henry dropped down his rifle for a moment and scratched at his head. His blonde hair was matted and covered in dirt to the point that it looked dark. He spit on the ground before looking over toward me. "Y'all are too stiff.

They haven't called for us yet. Who knows how long it will be." Henry pulled out a little flask and downed it.

"A bit early for drinking, Hen!" I shouted. Our volleys were becoming less prevalent as time went on. I had a bad feeling.

"Never too early," he said, holding it up.

"Give it to me," Levin said, reaching out a hand while holding his gaze forward.

Henry stared at him for a moment, then tossed it to him. Levin caught it with the practice of a well-known alcoholic and took a swig, before pushing it into my hand.

I shrugged and drank deep. The burning warmth of whiskey filled my chest and I coughed, almost dropping the flask.

Henry ran forward and grabbed it from my hand, breaking rank as he did, but no one seemed to care.

"Y'all should be ready," Jeremiah said. It was the first time the man had spoken in days. He was actually younger than we were, and he looked it. There was no trace of facial hair on his face, yet through the grime, his eyes were visible. A deep blue, so intimidating that I almost looked away. The boy was scary at times, as if he had lost all semblance of life or soul from within him. Nehemiah was his spitting image, the boy just stared downfield. He was a bit taller than his brother, whose side he never left. Jeremiah was always kind to him and spoke to him in low tones.

"What?" Henry said, turning and facing Jeremiah.

"Pickett's going to make his move soon." I was barely able to hear the boy, but the conviction in his voice gave me pause. "Be ready brother," he said, patting Nehemiah on the shoulder. His brother nodded in response.

"Why do you say that?" I asked, returning my gaze to the union troops that were lined up ahead of us.

"The cannon fire on their side is slowly fading away. Once it stops, we are free to charge, or at least march."

He was right, I hadn't noticed how quiet it had gotten on the other side. A ball formed in my stomach, it felt like a heavy rock. I didn't have a good feeling.

"There are also the crows," Jeremiah continued. "They are waiting. They must know something we don't."

He was right. Crows and buzzards, and all other manner of birds flew above us, circling as if we were dead deer. *The end was coming.*

"What do you—"

"Advance!" screamed a voice behind us, drowning out whatever Henry was in the middle of saying. Without a thought, we marched. Out of the corner of my eye, I caught Henry tossing his musket back up to his shoulder. It was for the best, we didn't need him dying for something stupid.

The unison of our footsteps in the grass was almost intoxicating. A steady drum that I could not get out of my head, along with the real drums. In truth, we were sure we had the city taken. Boy was that a mistake.

We quickly approached the union divisions. They stood on a hill above us. We were almost within charging distance, and once we charged, the battle would be won. *Then we can go home.* Without their artillery the Union troops wouldn't be able to deflect us. We would bust through their ranks, taking and killing all we could. Even though I didn't want to be in that army, I only had the thought of surviving in my mind. I didn't want to kill, but in a kill or be killed situation I would hate to be on the other side of my gun. The anticipation was killing me as we got closer, I waited for the order to fire, or charge. It didn't come.

"This is the beginning of the end, right? Then we can get back to the Forks?" Levin asked me. He was the only one close enough for me to hear.

"I think so. There is only so much that can be done, then we are ruled by this new nation. For better, or for worse, I reckon we'll find out quickly," I said. A new nation that I didn't think would look out for poor folk like us, but I had to keep moving. No matter what.

"Do you think Lucy is still waiting for me?" Levin grinned.

"I'm sure she's waiting to give you a hug when you get home. There's no way she isn't."

Levin looked directly at me and smiled. He was a good man, a kind one. I would've given anything to be back home shooting the shit with him.

"I'm hoping we can start a family once we're back," he said with a sheepish grin. "And you will be their favorite uncle."

I laughed with a true smile crossing my face for the first time in a long time.

He had been sweet on Lucy since we were kids, and of course she would be the one he was thinking of. In the face of death, we think about a lot of different people. For me it was Tootsie. The sweetest girl I had ever known.

My heart broke the day I lost her. When the Confederates invaded our town.

Thinking of that day so many decades later is painful. We had been pushed back to the courthouse. Many of the men had already been killed. My dad died in my arms in the lobby of the courthouse, which was really a small barn-like structure. Truthfully there was nothing special about it.

"Are we going to die, Easton?" Tootsie asked. Her black hair danced down her back. Her chocolate eyes almost made my heart skip a beat. She was sixteen, too young to be dealing with what we were. She stood maybe five feet tall, but as small as she was, she was ten times feistier.

We met when I accompanied my dad to the general store. Back then The Forks had only dirt roads, and a few small buildings on the main drag. My father was a gruff man, a classic mountain man; what people may call today a hillbilly. Even though we only lived a few miles out of town, Miles King was known to have a reputation of a tough customer and an alcoholic.

The previous day he had spent telling me what to do while he sat on the tractor drinking some Moonshine we had gotten from my uncle Philmon. He was the number one moonshiner in Wise County at the time, supplying most of the county and the surrounding towns with his good mountain water.

My father wasn't sober a day in his life, and that fateful day at the general store he was arguing with the owner. Saying something about how it was unfair to price seeds the way he was.

"This is robbery, Steven, and you know it," my father yelled as he slammed the door and turned to me, still waiting near the wagon. "He doesn't know what the fuck to price seeds at. We're ruined this time. Completely and totally." He sat down in the seat next to me and held his head in his hands.

I had never seen him be this way, never seen him show any type of emotion. Well not since we had to bury my momma. When we buried her the rain fell for days. As if the very world was crying for her. That's when my father started drinking, and he didn't stop till the day he died.

"Boy, you need to get out of here... You need to get up to Wise, maybe. Some place that will do more for you than here."

"What about you Pa?" I asked.

He smiled. "I don't have many years left but if I know you're okay, then I can die in peace." He gave my knee a squeeze, and that is when the horn blew.

Luckily, we kept our rifles in the cart and ran for the courthouse. The gunfire erupted far into the night. I laid my father's head down onto the old wood floor.

Someone embraced me from behind. "You okay?" Tootsie whispered.

"No..." I stood and took her in my arms. She was a tiny thing. When we pulled apart, I gently caressed her belly. "I didn't get to tell him... I didn't want him mad at me... We went against the gospel."

"What's done is done, my love. We can't get rid of this baby so easily."

"What if I'm not a good dad?" I asked. The quiet outside was beginning to unsettle me. There hadn't been a shot fired since they felled my father. I nodded down to him. "Like my dad?"

"You will be, and you will be nothing like him" She smiled, and a shot rang out. Tootsie jutted, and blood seeped from a wound in her chest, and she was gone. So was our son. I screamed into the night, unsure what to do now. With her gone, I wouldn't be able to do much. I had no reason to exist any longer. Anger is what fueled me from then on. Sadly, it still does.

I pushed the thoughts away. There was no need to think of her.

"Levin, You're the best man I have ever known. You will be a great dad."

"Thank you for that, Easton. It means a lot." He smiled his goofy smile at me, A shot rang out in the distance. *One of our cannons. It must be almost time.*

Levin exploded, his body turning into a slew of gore, with the smile still plastered across his face.

They weren't our cannons.

July 3rd, 1863: Death by The Thousands

The ranks broke quickly, as the image of Levin's smile danced in my mind. What the hell had happened? Did they not double check that the Union cannons were gone. Did they not care? I found out years later that the Union had tricked us. Turning us into a slow marching target. People screamed as the cannon balls slammed all around us. There was no way we could make it through everything. Even if we were close enough to take a shot, our charge was failing fast.

Yet, despite the break in ranks, our unit continued to move forward. With each shot I hoped that we would not be directly in the path. Somehow Levin was the only person we lost in the initial attack. I could only think of Levin and Lucy in those moments. Still think about them sometimes in the quiet moments here. How they will never live together, that the best person died, and I still lived. That truth breaks my heart, even writing this now. What the fuck am I to do...

I reckon my friends and I survived for a reason. I just wish it could have been possible to get us out quicker. Could we have fought more? Was Levin's death preventable? To this day I am unsure. However, I do know that if it was not for his death, I would not have learned what I have. Easton King would not have ended up on this path. Nope, instead I would have died in Gettysburg with Levin. Sometimes I wish I did.

"Charge!" A voice called over the cannon volleys, and we did. We were less than a hundred yards from where the Union soldiers stood. My friends ran next to me as we ran toward what I knew was certain death.

Henry bumped into me, yelling into my ear as we ran. "What do we do Easton? We're gonna die!"

At the moment I didn't have a response. A blue coat appeared directly in front of me. The darkness in his eyes unsettled me. He didn't care that I had been forced to fight. He didn't care that I didn't want to hurt him. His eyes told me that he wanted me to die.

I skidded to a stop, raised my rifle, and fired my only shot. Jeremiah and Henry must have done the same, because the three closest soldiers dropped to the ground. Their screams of pain echo in my mind, even today. Nehemiah stabbed and hit with a viciousness I had never seen in a person before and have never seen since.

With a section of the line broken, I turned and ran. "Boys, follow me," I called, hoping they could hear me over the screams and gunfire.

My friends showed up right beside me, and we ran past the line where the fighting was most prevalent. We ran behind them, racing past all the fighting soldiers, and none of them paid us any mind. Soldiers died all around us.

Ahead of us was a forest, if we could make it there, we might be able to hide and get out of the battle. It was either that or die. On the hill I could hear officers shouting. Gunfire slammed into the ground near us, but none hit. Everyone else was focused on the battle in front of them.

The woods were close. We were about to enter them, when something slammed into the back of my right knee, and I fell to the ground. The pain of a thousand hornets filled me. I screamed; sure I was going to die. But my friends turned around, pulled me to my feet, and ran with me.

Someone tackled us, knocking all three of us to the ground. Nehemiah must have been somewhere in the foray. Our guns were gone, lost somewhere in the mud below us. My heart slammed in my chest as a man got atop me. His greasy beard tickled my face as he punched my mouth. Something cracked and a warmth ran down my face. The viciousness was worse than I could have ever expected. It was as if the man had been filled with a bloodlust, he had no thought but of my death.

His calloused hands wrapped around my neck.

"You don't know what you're doing!" the man screamed. "Your blood will fill the world; the final sacrifice is here. We *need* you."

What the hell? Is what I wanted to ask, but he wasn't giving me enough breath to speak. He laughed as he continued to choke me. Where were my friends? There was no way they had already been killed, the man couldn't have been that fast, right?

"You're mine!" the man screamed, as the dots filled my vision. My mind was fading. His face transformed into that of a skeleton. His eyes were a deep yellow. "It's the only way to win the war."

Something slammed into the back of the man's head, and he fell atop of me. His hands loosened and I coughed as I tried to fill my lungs with oxygen. As my vision cleared someone pulled the man off of me.

I slowly sat up, the pain returning to my leg. It was horrible, I could tell I had almost died. The battle still raged around us. I glanced over, and Jermiah had a bayonet to the man's neck.

I should have wanted to kill him, but a curiosity ran over me. "Don't," I croaked.

Jermiah looked back at me. Confusion filled his eyes.

"Take him with us," I said, as Henry helped me stand.

"He just tried to kill you," Jeremiah said, pushing the bayonet into the man's neck. A bead of blood popped out from the compressed skin.

"Yes, but he said something to me, and I want to know more."

Jermiah stared into my eyes, his look very accusing, as if I was making a bad decision, and in truth I might have been.

Jermiah shouldered his gun and picked the man up. "Nehemiah, hold him." His brother appeared out of the woods and grabbed the man. We were right outside of the forest. "If he kills us this is on you," he said as he walked into the darkening woods.

"I know."

Henry didn't say anything, he just helped me into the woods. Just inside the tree line, he sat me down and investigated my leg. There we watched the battle rage, but at least we were free. As long as neither army found us, we would be okay. If only we knew that the man we took would change all of our lives.

We watched as the confederate line fell apart. They were in active retreat out of fear, each soldier running for themselves. The charge had failed and we watched into the wee hours of the morning. Our friend who had tried to take my life was now tied up, Nehemiah watching over him. Yet he never woke. He had to have knocked him hard, but with Jeremiah's strength I wasn't surprised.

Memories of Levin passed over me. That smile haunted me every time I closed my eyes. The horrors of war changed me, and on the eve of another I am glad that I am too old to serve again. I cannot rightly say that I am moved by the great war. Yet the reports remind me of the times during what is now known as the American Civil War. Despite there being no civility around it. None at all.

We watched as people were blown to bits. We watched as the killing fields were investigated. As the poor souls we stabbed to death or shot for playing dead.

We watched as both armies disappeared, and light returned to the sky.

I could not sleep, the demons of the day before haunted everything I did. I can only hope that I will die as Levin did, with a smile, and with love. It was all I could hope for in the future.

Tootsie, God did I miss her.

As the light danced across the hills, the full carnage of the day before came into view. Bodies glittered in the sunlight covered in their own blood. The ones who had avoided the killings last night screamed. The sound was almost too much for us to handle, yet we still watched. *I should've been there.*

A murder of crows circled high overhead, ready for their feast. God, how could this have happened? Thousands of men died, and for what? Truthfully it was a waste.

I forced myself to stand.

"We need to get moving," I whispered.

"Where?" Henry asked.

"Hopefully home."

Henry smiled at that.

"We got to," my voice caught and I had to take a moment to compose myself. "We got to tell Lucy about Levin."

We all dropped our eyes for our friend. He was the best of us, and I wonder now if the events that followed his death would have happened if he was there to talk sense into us all. Would I have done any of it? Would I have let the odd man live?

Part of me wishes I could have lived that life, or that the cannon ball would have got me. I could be at peace. Yet it did not, and that made all the difference. I chose my path and will follow it to the end of everything if I can. Even if it never heals the hole shot through my soul.

" Let's go," I said, gesturing for Jeremiah to pick up our prisoner.

" I know I am the strongest, but must I always carry things?" Jeremiah said, a smile across his face.

" If I didn't have the bum leg I would, but I got shot! I'm a war hero now."

Nehemiah pushed past us and picked up the prisoner.

"Are you sure?" Jeremiah asked.

Nehemiah nodded.

We ventured deeper into the woods. Each of us prayed that we wouldn't run into any of the armies. Lucky for us we didn't, at least not at first.

July 12th, 1863

We had not been able to move far. Our companion turned hostage had finally woken up, yet he didn't speak to us. He only stared into the distance and took food when we gave it. Luckily Henry was able to keep his musket and hunted for us. It had been a hard week or so. I was starting to wonder if running had really been worth it.

Granted, we hadn't been attacked any more, nor could our "friend" do anything to hurt us. For now, we were safe. We let the man stay by himself, which was sad in its own right, the man was raving when he tried to kill me, and he just stopped speaking. I only heard the man utter a single sentence since we took him. He would repeat it over and over under his breath.

"Ruined it," he would whisper. Even late at night when I was trying to sleep, I would hear him speaking to himself. Always those same words as I fell asleep. The man was a lunatic; it was the only solution. *If only I had not met that man.*

During the day it was hot. So hot that we had to take off parts of our uniforms to stay cool. Water had become scarce and food wasn't easy to come by. Even with Henry hunting, he eventually ran out of shots, and we didn't see any animals from that day on. We hadn't eaten in three or so days at this point, which meant we were on the brink of collapse. Every once in a while, we would find a berry or two, but they wouldn't fill us at all. It would just make our hunger worse.

The man watched us try to eat the variety of nuts I had gathered. When I bit into them, they were bitter, I spit them out and he laughed, and muttered. He continued to be a crazy man.

As that night fell however, something changed. Jeremiah and Henry were asleep. Nehemiah stood over our prisoner, I had only seen him sleep once or twice, and that was when his brother told him he could. I had taken the first watch. Granted I did not know what I would do if someone came. Especially with no weapon except for the bayonet, we had taken off the discarded musket.

" Come here, my friend," a gruff voice whispered. I jumped, afraid of who it may be.

" Who's there?" I called. My voice echoed through the woods that surrounded us. During the day they were beautiful, stretching out as far as I could see. At night however they were like pillars in the night. Standing high in hopes of destroying us. No, that couldn't be right, but it is what I felt. Like people were watching me from deep within.

"Kid, the time is coming. You don't know what you have done."

The man's voice echoed behind me.

I tried to ignore him. Why was the man speaking out now? He had spent days ignoring any of our questions, and now something had changed. I just could not put a finger on it.

"Boy, you got any food?" The man asked.

My stomach rumbled. " There is no food," I muttered. Truly speaking to the man for the first time.

"Oh, well, come here kid." He coughed. I could not tell if it was fake or not, but I turned. Thinking back on it, it was as if the man had a grasp on me that I couldn't figure out or put a finger on. I found myself worrying about him despite my not wanting to care. Before I knew it, I was crouched in front of him. Nehemiah was nowhere to be seen, which now strikes me as *off* when I think back on it, but in the moment I didn't notice.

Blood sat at the corners of his lips.

"What's wrong?" I asked putting a hand out.

"Don't touch me!" He yelled. His voice echoed through the woods, breaking all silence.

I jumped back and glanced over my shoulder at my friends. They didn't move, nor did Nehemiah come out from wherever he had disappeared to. Good I did not need them causing trouble right now.

"Sorry," the man continued. "I hurt; I don't want to hurt anymore."

There were tears shining in his eyes. The pale moonlight reflected through them. They were a cat's yellow. Which wasn't right. The man had brown eyes in the daylight. I remembered that much, despite the hunger.

I jumped back.

"The light is changing. We failed."

I stared at him in confusion.

"You don't know what you have done?"

The man was not making any sense. The guy had to be crazy.

"What's your name?"

The man only stared at me. Was he really going to go dumb on me again?

"Simon. Simon Monroe. Leader of the Men Who Wait. We watch the one in yellow, who stands beyond our own world. Locked behind the Veil."

"What are you talking about?"

"His power will change the world; it will make us more than we are. The sacrifice should have been enough, but you ruined it. Not enough people died, he will never return. The rest of the order is gone as well. It's only me..." Tears ran down his face. I watched as Simon's mind was cracking at the seams. "I'm sorry, there was just so much that could be done through those who lie beyond. Simon smiled. His yellow teeth peeked out of his black beard.

"I can show you where they are, maybe all isn't lost."

"Why would I follow a madman?" I asked. Truthfully, at that moment I thought about killing the man. Ending his damn suffering, but his yellow eyes unnerved me. *He can't be normal.*

"You can see Tootsie again," Simon said with an evil smile. "Your baby too. All things can be brought back from the other side with the right power."

My heart dropped, how did he know about them? There was no damn way, no way at all. Was it possible for some random Union soldier to be telling the truth? Was it possible for him to know so much about me? The questions continued to flood my mind as the fear surged through my veins. The man was mad, and my mind told me that, but... What if he was right?

If he was right, then I could see her again.

"You mean back to life?" I asked, knowing it could not be possible.

"Yes," Simon's smile unnerved me, but the memory of Tootsie was too strong. Something did not feel right about his words, but if I could see Tootsie again, I would do anything. I made a decision that changed the direction of my life. Even though it went against everything I had ever believed in.

"What do we need to do?"

August 1st, 1863

"This man is leading us on a wild good chase and has been for a fortnight," Jeremiah grumbled. He had been complaining for days while Nehemiah just walked along with us, his eyes fixed upon the back of that blue coat.

Simon walked in front of us; he had been moving us back and forth throughout the forest as if it was some type of maze. Honestly, I wasn't sure where we had been. Luckily, we kept finding already dead animals throughout the woods. Did we find it odd? Sure, but we needed to survive. I followed Simon without fretting.

"Where are we going?" Henry asked, He was huffing. Something was not right about him. He was getting less lucid the longer we were in the woods, and the longer we walked. His breathing got heavier and his steps less coordinated. I had to help pick him up multiple times despite my own issues. I was already using a walking stick myself, and the wound in the back of my knee stank, as if I was decaying, but I felt good. Not that it meant much, but I wasn't feeling any pain.

Jeremiah, on the other hand, was unfazed by everything. He kept moving, never leaving his brother's side. The farther away we went from civilization, the more he seemed to mellow. He loved the woods, always had since we were kids, but something was different this time. I had never seen him afraid in the slightest. His sense of direction was top tier, yet Jeremiah had paled significantly. Which scared me. I had never seen him scared in the woods, but for whatever reason, the fear fell off him—entering the air and giving it a feeling I cannot describe. It was as if the very air around us shook.

"Is anyone else getting cold?" Henry asked, visibly shaking.

"It is getting a little cool," I said.

Jeremiah agreed.

Simon had led us somewhere that we didn't know. We were not even sure if we were in Pennsylvania anymore. Simon stumbled back and forth.

"On we go, and on we go. On we go, ho ho, we go." He repeated the phrase over and over again. Even when I got close to him it seemed like he didn't remember we were following him.

"Simon, where are you taking us?" I asked, my heart thumping in my chest. Maybe I shouldn't have let him lead us so deep into the woods.

"Their home... Their home... but they are being tricky. I'm waiting for the words." Simon was almost all skin and bones at this point, and I wondered if he was even sane now. Lack of food can do something to a man. Not to mention they hadn't had water in days.

"That doesn't answer the question," Jeremiah said. Pulling out what had to be his last cigarette and lighting it. Again, Nehemiah only stared at the man.

I still cannot figure out where he hid the smoke. It should have been easy to find among everything, and why he had not shared was beyond me. Granted, I did not smoke but the thought would have been nice.

"We're almost there!" Simon shouted before cackling "The truth is near."

A gun cocked. Henry and I both shot around. Nehemiah held a revolver, but he wasn't aiming for either of us. He was aiming for Simon.

No, I could not let this happen.

"Nehemiah," I shouted, putting myself between him and the madman.

"King, I'll kill you. I'm not going to die of starvation out here."

"He's leading us–"

"In circles."

"Yes! We are so close!" Simon yelled. I glanced over my shoulder; the man was on all fours digging like a dog. My heart dropped. Could this man be truly mad? Was Tootsie not a possibility?

"Step out of the way," Nehemiah said, cocking the gun. "I'll get us out of here, but this man is nothing more than a feral being. He needs to die. It is the only mercy."

Jeremiah stood, looking back and forth between us. "Neh," tears welling in the poor man's eyes. "You had a gun this whole time? We could have used it for food."

Henry pushed Jeremiah away, his eyes filled with desperation and betrayal. I hadn't paid attention to my old friend like I should have. The man was so thin his clothes hung off of him as if he was wrapped in the uniform. The heat must've dehydrated him as his face had sunk in, despite his small amount of stubble. He had changed so much in these few weeks. How had I ignored it? I watched as his heartbeat in his chest and fell to my knees.

"I needed something in case the mad man went after me," Nehemiah said to Henry, before pointing the revolver at Simon again, who was still digging away. His pale eyes fell upon me and I froze. A disappointment looked from them. "You just now realize what you have done to our friend. He can barely stand."

He was right. Henry stood in front of me as if he was a leaning tower. The tall, proud man had mostly fallen away.

" Lord, what have I done?" I stepped back.

"You're gonna let him kill that man. Didn't you say Simon was our only answer?" A rage echoed from deep within Henry's chest.

Jeremiah had flanked his brother, ready to do what must be done, I was outnumbered at this point. I stared at Simon, who was about a foot into the ground, still digging. Mud caked his body as blood flew with each pull of dirt.

How had I not seen it before? Was my need for the baby and Tootsie really that huge that I would follow this wretch of a man?

The tears that were pooled in my eyes fell, and I screamed.

After composing myself I said only two words. "Do it."

Nehemiah nodded and pulled the trigger. Everything slowed down for a moment. As the gun fired, Henry jumped, knocking into Simon. Blood flew into the air followed by a scream.

What had I allowed? Murder. It could only be murder.

Before I could take in who had been shot, the ground rumbled and shifted, opening up as if it was a mouth ready to consume us.

Without any ground beneath us, we all fell. The blood danced in the air as darkness took over the sky.

August 1st. 1863 (continued)

I thought I would never see again. Someone moaned from a spot that could not have been far from me.

"Here, we're here!" Simon shouted from far away, I thought, but couldn't be sure as the cavern echoed around us. My heart thumped in my chest at a speed I had never felt before.

There were drips and scurrying around me.

"What happened?" I asked, mainly to myself. I was unsure if the others were there, or if they were still alive. For all I knew they were still up on the surface, leaving me alone in the dark.

I sat up, rubbing my back, warm blood running down my leg where the bullet wound had reopened.

"Damn, that sucked," Jeremiah said from next to me. Or was it Nehemiah? After hearing them speak I am not sure which one was which. Especially with the backbone that Nehemiah showed. It was so much more like Jeremiah. He was closer than I thought and I almost jumped at his voice.

"It's here! It's here! It's here!" Simon cackled in the distance.

In that moment flames shot up around us, they brought the cave to life in a yellowish light.

I stood with some effort. This was more than a cave. It was a chamber with a high ceiling leading into a darkness in front of us.

"Come! Come!" Simon jumped like a monkey.

What had happened to the poor man? He was completely different from when he tried to kill me. His yellow eyes danced in the darkness.

"Where's Henry?" I asked.

"Don't know," Jeremiah said as he holstered his revolver. No, it was Nehemiah, all these years later and I am still unsure which it was.

Below us was what looked like a puddle. I bent down and touched it. It was tacky. Blood. That was all it could be. Where had Henry gone?

The puddle moved toward the darkness before the blood disappeared.

Our footsteps echoed as we walked toward where Simon's voice was coming from. The room moved out in front of us. It was never ending.

I stopped for a moment and looked over my shoulder. "Where is Jeremiah?"

"I am Jeremiah,"

So, I had been right initially.

"Then where is your brother?"

A tear formed in the big man's eye. "I do not know."

The change that had fallen over Jeremiah was one I could not overlook. It was as if he had become more brash than usual, then more reserved. The man was making no sense.

Behind us was a light, bright and white. "Do you think he is in there?" I asked.

"If so, then he is one." Jeremiah turned. "He is lost, just like Henry. I do not think it is wise to go back though. There definitely isn't a way out." He clapped me on the shoulder. "Come."

And I did.

The flames kicked on after each step. The colors changed as we walked. From yellow, to purple, to red, a deep green, and finally a light blue.

After the last fire kicked in, the room opened up. A white light filled it; there were five tunnels in front of us. Each shone in one of the different colors. Each one had words I couldn't make out at the top of each corridor.

A body sat at the center of the room.

Henry. How could he be here?

I ran forward. Blood pooled around my friend's body. It had to be all of his blood. There were grooves in the carved floor that ran down each hallway, disappearing into the dark colored mists.

The blood soaked into each, moving toward the mists.

Simon danced as he watched the blood.

"Yes, yes! The lord is coming!" He danced at the front of the yellow tunnel. The blood finally stopped.

"No, no." Simon fell to the floor crying. "This isn't right. Not right at all."

I walked forward and reached to touch him. Simon jumped as if I had shot him or was going to kill him.

Simon looked up at me, his eyes had paled.

"He died too quickly. Far too quick," Simon whispered, slamming a hand down on the stone beneath our feet.

It was not raw stone; however, this had been refined and laid. Like bricks that were put every few feet, or a castle. This place was different, very different.

Jeremiah stood back away from us. He was not willing to partake in the man's madness, or he was grieving his twin. Either way, something had changed within him. Part of me wanted to do as he did, but... but I needed to know if it was possible.

"Tell me. Can I really bring her back?"

"The six have many powers, they can bring back just as they can take away. Blue, I hear the blue can resurrect."

"Who did you hear this from?" I asked, pulling Simon to his feet and dusting him off. My hope being since he was calming down, I could maybe get real answers.

"I only answer to the yellow. He brings power and lust. Red fills those with fear, destruction laying in his mist. Purple wants freedom no matter what the rest say. Black brings death, that's his only want, but he we all reach in time. Finally, green is of disease. He will take those with a plague. Last is the blue, who is chaos itself."

Jeremiah laughed behind me. "You can't be taking this man seriously, Easton."

But I was.

"Continue please." I gestured to Simon, who stood completely to his full height. "We need more blood. The Old Gods come through sacrifice, sometimes you see them as nightmares, or the darkness of the world, yet they wait. There are more than the five, but the five are the ones who are in this specific spot. They wait, My king waits within his tunnel." He pointed into the yellow mist. "We need to kill him!" Simon pointed at Jeremiah. "If we do, the power will be ours!"

A gun clicked behind me.

"Jeremiah, don't," I said. I was not going to let him take away the hope that Simon was giving me. I could not let this end this way. Not if there was a chance, I could see her again. " What does blue do?"

"He has the power to take and give life."

I swear to this day my heart stopped for a moment, his honesty was palpable. The look in his eyes said it all.

"If anyone is dying, it is him," Jeremiah said, his voice filled with venom.

Simon squealed and hid behind me. I turned to face my oldest friend and sighed as I saw the cocked gun pointed just over my shoulder. That he would go this far broke my heart. He was my closest friend. Surely, he could understand. I know he lost his brother, but we could bring him back.

"If you could see your parents again, would you risk it? If you could bring back Nehemiah, would you?" I asked. A chill shot through the air. My very marrow turned to ice.

"I... Easton, they're gone," he said, the gun dropping a little.

Jeremiah had lost his parents at a very young age, from what he told me. The only things he remembered about them was their warmth and smiles. Now that he had lost his brother, what type of friend was I to do this to him again? I was manipulating the man based on his fears and worries—his grief. Nothing good could come of this, yet I knew I needed to. An energy was washing over me. It filled me with a want I couldn't explain.

"Old friend, I have the chance to see her again, and my unborn child. I would kill for that."

Jeremiah moved the gun toward me. "I guess you need a lesson. Can you really think of bringing them back from the grave? If I brought my parents back as revenants. What would they think?"

I gulped, was he really contemplating it? Could he do what I was thinking of doing myself? He had always been the best of all my friends. A man's man. Now he was the only one left, but he was a good man. A very good man, almost to a fault. I smiled; he had always had a good conscience since we were kids. Never wanting to cause any trouble and that was always great. Even if he made me take the sweets back to the general store in town.

God dammit. I could not decide what to do and that scared me. Philosophically there was a lot here, at least I realize it now. That it was more than just the good and bad. Even if that's how I saw the world. The shades of Grey were what made the world a more beautiful place, a scarier place, a heart-breaking place.

Yet I know now the madness that took me. The cough that pains me in this God forsaken place was enough. It continues to remind me of the mistakes I made.

I don't know if anyone will read this, or if the madness I fall into will take me. If it is a family member please turn back. You do not know what you are calling up here. You don't know at all. If you take too much time thinking about what you want, you can lose your place in the world. Even as people like John Wright fought to tame the hills. It doesn't mean that the darkness is something to fall into. If a Godly man like Marshall Taylor could fall, any of us could, and that risk is one I wish I didn't take.

November 24th, 1972

Simon sighed. For some reason he had always skimmed through those passages, but part of him wondered if they were always there. Had he made a mistake with the ritual? Was attempting it a complete fucking bust from the beginning? He reckoned that his grandfather had messed up everything. Or had the Sword family done that? Either way, it seemed that the entities that beckoned from beyond the veil. If only he could grasp that power...He had killed the entire town to get Shelia back.

She will come if you do what is needed. You didn't succeed, but plenty of other opportunities await. You called but failed. The vampiric dark was not your intention, I assume.

"No, it wasn't."

Your grandfather laid the groundwork. Why not just keep going. I can help you.

"Who are you?"

The mad man said much. The king in yellow was a misnomer. His power wasn't there in the book, it was the power of the Crawler, those vampiric forces surrounded by mist. But I can help you.

"Who are you?"

My name doesn't matter, but my power is what you seek. I can save Shelia.

"My wife?"

Yes, indeed. But there are risks. I entered your mind long ago; you opened up to me. Now Freedom shall come.

A coolness filled his body, a purple light pulsing around him.

Unleash us and the power is yours. Deep purple eyes blinked at him.

Simon jumped. Had he gone after the wrong power the whole time?

No, the Crawler can do it, but so can I. The nameless mist that surrounds him makes it seem like it's not possible, but...

"Why didn't grandpa know?"

You said you read the book, yes? There was a slight hiss to the voice.

It was unlike the voice he had heard before. The one that guided him from the book. Got him to transfer the pamphlet into the Jackson woman's house, drove her mad... drove him to kill his sons.

Blood is blood. Bring me a vessel, and all the power will be yours. Finish your grandfather's work. Read what was done, and why things were set up this way. That will provide the answer.

The eyes blinked and disappeared.

Simon nearly screamed. What in the hell had happened. Was that thing really trying to control him? Or what was its purpose? What did he mean by a vessel? It must've been important. Simon didn't want to read any longer, but against his will his hand reached out. It grabbed the book and slid it open. *God help me.*

August 1st 1863...again

I stared down the barrel of that gun. Unable to truly see the truth. My mind was fracturing, it seemed, and I hated it. My best friend had a gun to my head, ready to kill me. I never expected it to go this way.

Did I really need to do this? To find Tootsie? To return her?

The lights rainbowed around us.

As an aside, I don't know why I am writing this down, but the information could be so detrimental to everything I have done. To everyone. Looking back now, I know I messed up. Big time, bigger than I had ever done before. Don't make me write this... Yet Caeben's voice, the one who crawls echoes in my mind. Filling me with thoughts pushing me to keep moving my pen, because if I do, he will return them to me. Even where I failed. He said, "You will succeed, my grandson," is what he said.

But listen, please. Whoever you are... don't follow what he commands me to write all these years later. I can feel him consuming me, but my hope is that you will not do the same.

Simon stared at the warning for a moment and turned the page.

"I need to see Tootsie again," I whispered, staring straight into the dark hole of the gun.

"So, you have made your choice?" Jeremiah cocked the gun and depressed the trigger.

Behind me, I could hear Simon dance with joy. He was completely intangible now. The world slowed, and as I dropped to the ground, a gun shot rang out. I waited for pain to fill me, but it never did. The shot echoed in the darkness followed by a rumbling. Rocks danced down around us, as Jeremiah screamed. I looked up in time to see the rocks fall in front of him.

"What have you done?" I yelled. " What have you done!" Fear slammed into the forefront of my mind.

"I'm sorry," is all I heard Jeremiah say as he disappeared from sight.

I turned around; Simon was dead. The bullet had struck him right between the eyes. His blood ran through the indention.

It welled up, heading down the blue corridor. The lights dimmed as the corridors were blocked. Only pale blue was left. All the blood funneling down it.

A voice echoed in my mind.

Follow.

Against my own volition I walked until the blue mist-like substance surrounded me. I couldn't see anything; I couldn't hear anything. Simon's body had disappeared somewhere behind me, I'm sure it is still there somewhere. He never got to see his king. Never got to see anything but the darkness of the void.

I fell to my knees and screamed; claustrophobia fell across me. Where was Jeremiah and what had he done? Had he ended everything for me? I coughed; at the time I wanted to say it was because of the mist that surrounded me, but I know differently now, sitting in this sanatorium, surrounded by the coughing of others. I should have seen it, but I didn't. My mind was broken, lusting for Tootsie.

I stood and continued to walk forward. A door squeaked open in front of me as I took in everything. The mist cleared and the Crawler was there hunched on his throne, where he had been stuck for so long.

Its pale blue face looked up at me, releasing a sigh from its sightless eyes, the sockets were deep and unseeing. I could only think of where his eyes had gone. His body pulsed and moved shifting forms but always eyeless.

"You dare approach me." It smiled, with teeth black as night.

My blood pulsed in my ears, as it stood from its throne.

The being was tall and slender, covered in a fine peach fuzz-like hair that shifted with its form. It was as if he couldn't keep his shape for long at all. It pulsed some more, before settling with the head of what may have been an eyeless vulture.

"I was attempting to take a form more cohesive with your feeble brain. Your mind can't handle me, or the others. Yet freedom is what beckons us all. You are the only one to approach us. I think the King is the only one who has had a visitor in a millennium. Are you the vessel I have sought?"

I fell to the floor, cowering away from the monster in front of me. I have now come to know that he is an Old God. Older than our world, older than the Christian God himself. Fear ran through me and still does as I remember him.

Even if he still speaks to me, complaining of my failures and broken promises, from when I killed Jeremiah, and turned him into the spawn of a monster, but not the vessel he wished for. God, it wasn't right, but I wanted her... Sometimes things are not what they seem.

In a blink he stood in front of me. "You will release me, by bringing me back to the world above. To savage the masses." He smiled, grabbing me with his cold hands. "I can give and take life. That is all I want. Fill me with the power of the dead and I shall grant you your loved one back."

"You want me to kill in your name?" I asked as he pulled me to my feet.

"You will bring me back through the energy of the lost, and the damned."

"And if I don't?"

"Then you leave. But I think you will have a hard time getting out of here without me."

" How can I believe you?"

The Crawler raised his hand, turning to ash in an instant, and pulsing through and around me. A figure appeared in the distance.

"Easton," a voice called, no it could not be her, but it was.

She came into the light as the monster returned and pointed.

I ran forward without thinking.

Tootsie held something close to her chest. "Easton, how are we here?"

I hugged her and my son, tears running down my face. "I thought you were gone."

"It was so dark," she began, but then exploded in a geyser of gore. I screamed as the monster came into my vision and embraced me.

"I am Caeben, and I will bring her back if you do what is needed. Bring me back."

Ice filled my veins. Creating what I could only describe as a feeling of loss. Something broke in my mind. I could not take it anymore. I was consumed only by the idea that I needed to see Tootsie again.

"What must I do?" I whispered.

"Kill." He sunk his teeth into my neck and I screamed. His voice echoed in my mind. "Kill those who wait in the dark, the ones who fill you with dread, kill them all. With each death in my name, I get closer."

"Is that all?"

Caeben sank his teeth farther into my throat. My warm blood ran down my neck. "Eons ago, my eyes were taken. My power to kill with a glance, is now gone. You must find them, or your family will forever be cursed."

"That was not our deal!" I screamed.

Caeben laughed as he flowed around me, blood and dust, darkness and light. Had Jeremiah been right? Could this have been a bad idea? Another click echoed in my head, it felt as if it was splitting into pieces. My body burned as a darkness filled me.

My arms flew in every direction, throwing blood, my guts slurred out and wrapped around my throat like a noose, pulling all life from me. I attempted to scream but couldn't.

"You are part of me now Easton, kill and make them with my blood. My minions shall rise, and blood shall fill the sky of the world. But one man works against us."

As my body continued to separate from my mind I whispered. "Who?"

"Jeremiah Sword."

October 1900

I plopped onto the cold earth, unable to move. My heart is beating hard in my chest. Time seemed different now, the snow beneath me should have chilled my body but it did not. I sat up and looked around. I was on the street. One like no other I had ever seen. On the ground next to me sat a paper.

October 29, 1900.

No, that could not be possible. How could I have lost so much time.

"Time passes differently beneath. You must get started," Caeben's voice whispered. I stood, and my head spun. The hill on which I stood was higher than any other.

My body panged and I turned. The pain was pushing me in a direction I did not know, pushing me through the trees. I ran, moving faster and faster, unable to control my body. A man stood in a field brushing away snow to make a path across it. I did not understand why, maybe it was for the cows.

The man looked up and spotted me, a smile crossing his face.

I stopped as the man waved.

"Are you lost my friend?"

I nodded, not wanting to speak.

"Where you get those clothes? War's been done for decades."

I did not care that much, but a part of me... maybe the old me, was glad that the war was over. It meant I could return to Three Forks in peace.

Without a second thought, when the man looked down, I ran at him, with a speed I did not have before, a mist dancing around me, and I then was upon him. Tearing, ripping. Drinking in his blood, before stabbing my fingers into him and pushing my own blood into him. The man bloated, before erupting in a shower of blood.

He did not have a chance to scream. I was invigorated, feeling more alive than ever as the man's body, blood and all, disappeared into the crust of the earth.

" How many do I have to kill?" I asked, without expecting an answer.

Six, and after that, for the ritual to take effect on your friend Jeremiah... in the time you were gone he found my eyes. Or I think he did, he has been driven mad.

"Why can't you see him as you did me? "

Because he never met me. I am powerful, but it doesn't last. Run

I ran; I did not even tell my body to do so. I just ran.

October 31st 1900: Two Days Later

It did not take me long to get to my destination. With the power that filled my body now, I was quite confident I could do anything.

Tootsie, I'm coming.

She was always at the forefront of my mind, even when the Crawler came, breaking into my mind like a monster in the night. Even as I did unspeakable things. However, I could not bring myself to confront my friend without talking to him first, and that's what I did that snowy Halloween night.

Jermiah had taken up residence in a cabin outside of what was left of Three Forks. Granted, the town had been growing again, so it did not surprise me in the least. I trudged through the trees to get there. Hoping against hope that he would have the eyes and that would be the end of it.

As I ran, I found an ice-covered creek. In it I caught a glimpse of myself. I expected to see the strapping man I had once been. But that was not the case. In his place stood a grizzled man. White hair and beard, eyes of a light blue despite the color originally being brown. It surprised me, and part of me couldn't believe it was me. I still do not know what I was expecting, but it definitely was not the old man in front of me.

Pain filled my body, and I fell to my knees, trying not to scream. I was within sight of the cabin, but whatever had come over me was too much. My leg throbbed so badly that I did not know what to do.

Old pains return to my friend, you only have a taste of the power, and I suspect something in that cabin seems to nullify the abilities I granted you. But maybe this will work in your favor.

"What do you mean?"

You'll be decrepit and unsuspecting. A perfect trick for that friend of yours.

"He won't recognize me."

No... but that's okay right? Maybe he won't kill you on sight then.

The elder being had a point. I stood, and pain exploded in my leg. Next to me was, oddly enough, a nice stick that had been slammed down into the snow.

I picked it up and leaned against it as I made my way to the cabin. The walking stick helped immensely, and I made it to the front door without a problem.

I raised my hand and knocked.

The door cracked open, and a snarled green eye stared back at me.

And I just smiled.

"Nope, you will not enter, old man," Jeremiah muttered, a gun poking out of the space between the door and the wall.

"Jeremiah, are you not happy to see me? Don't you recognize me, of all people, old friend?" I said, putting a hand against the door.

Realization lined his face, before it turned into anger. "Leave, Easton. I don't know how you're alive, but I want nothing to do with you." He cocked the gun.

"I'll know you have been working against him. He wants you; don't you know that?"

"Bringing those things back won't work. Look what they have done to others, the writers and poets have gone mad. Seeing these monsters has destroyed them... your eyes. They are nothing."

He pulled the trigger and a pain filled my gut as I fell to the ground. Despite the pain, I laughed, the moon staring down upon me as the door slammed. Did he really think he could do this to me, of all people? No, and I was going to end this. But it might take some time. I drug myself away into the woods and became one with him, for a moment.

His hands danced across me. His blood filled me, and thus I was healed as his specter held me tight. I am unsure of who it may be—the voice was different from the Crawlers. The mist danced around me; a smile crossed the specter's face. One word danced on his lips, "Kill."

November 20th, 1900

The sixth girl was the easiest to take. She squirmed in my grasp as I ran through the woods. She was no more than five years old. I was almost to the spot when she bit my hand. Pain ran through me, but it was nothing compared to what I had felt before. When I was getting ready for the kill, my limp would disappear. It was as if I was a whole new man.

I finally arrived at the clearing. A single hole sat at the center of it. From Caeben's monologues in my head it seemed as if it was a route to him. It would be where I placed the eyes as well, which were still in Jeremiah's possession.

I tossed the girl in the hole. It was deeper than she was tall, and I smiled down at her as she screamed.

"Where's Momma?" She wailed.

"She is coming, my dear," I said in my sweetest voice. "She will be here soon. Just drink this as you wait."

I tossed her a canteen filled with my blood. It was an important part of the ritual. If she did not have the blood, then Caeben could not take her.

The child took a sip; like I said, she was easy to catch, the ones playing in the woods always were.

The girl spit out the blood.

"Eww." She wailed, holding the canteen up in the air.

I slid my revolver out of my holster and cocked it, pointing it directly at the girl. "Be good and drink, little one."

Tears ran down her face as darkness filled the woods. A blue mist rose from the grave as the girl drank, the same color I had seen in the cave. But the Crawlers' voice seemed more distant with each kill, and I didn't understand why. He hadn't spoken to me in weeks.

She caught and tossed the bottle away.

"Can I go home now?" She asked. I stared at her for a moment while I waited. For a very long time she just stared at me.

I was waiting for the word.

Kill. Caeben's voice whispered. It was now no more than the wind. A smile formed on my face, and I pulled the trigger. My laughter echoed through the woods, as the girl sank into the ground, sucked away into the darkness of the earth.

Gunshots echoed behind me and I jumped. My limp became more pronounced again. I leaned on my stick as I approached a tree. In the darkness I saw movement, and torches behind the person who was running.

No, no, no,

I watched as the man screamed. It was a voice I recognized. Jeremiah. He was on the run. No, it happened too quickly. I hadn't even confirmed where the eyes were, but if I had to guess, Jeremiah would have them on him.

That was my only hope. A smile formed on my face, and he was coming to the spot, yes that was good, better than good, it was perfect. I watched as he fell into the hole, and I slowly approached. Grabbing the shovel, I kept next to the grave. Now it would be his forever grave.

I looked down into the grave. He was broken in a way I could not imagine. His body was torn in different directions.

"Easton," he whispered.

I smiled at him, I'm sure I said something, but I could not remember what I muttered as I pushed dirt atop of him.

Pops echoed through the woods, as the mob got to me.

"I got him," I said, then laughed. The others helped me finish the burial.

I sat on the ground staring at the makeshift grave. Everyone else was gone, I was just waiting for my Lord. He would reward me for this. I just did not know how long it would take.

Caeben screamed through my mind for the first time. *You idiot. He didn't have them... the ritual. What have you done?*

"But I brought you the bodies."

I only needed the eyes.

"Then who?"

The ground shook around me, and I ran, at least I ran as best I could. He only chastises me now. As I sit here writing it all down, he laughs at me. I have moments where I am lucid, and others where I am broken. My mind is in shambles. But I must write what I have learned before it's too late. I still don't know how things got so messed up, but they did.

Something else spoke to you. It's the only way.

First, I regret killing my friend. How could I do that to a man who loved me for so long. Second, he is now a proper time bomb. A voice whispers in my head about a descendant, and how he will bring forth the power of the Crawler, and his vampiric dark, or was it him? Had I been manipulated by another being? I cannot be sure.

I have spent the years since finding out what I can about these old deities. Their power, their wants, and what they have done.

My mind only tells me one thing. *The King will save and bring back the Dark.* I am unsure how they are connected, but maybe there are multiple deities within each color. Is the mist different? *She will return.* I smile at the thought.

The powers as far as I know are as follows. This is from conversations with so many people before I was confined to the sanatorium. The information is true, as far as I know. But take the truth within my words with a grain of salt, Simon. Please, it might not be worth it.

The Blue/The Crawler, perched upon a darkened throne he waits to return from his prison. Which has pained him, confined by the darkness, stuck within the blue mist, every moment is agony to him. Eyes that sparkle in the night will bring you forever life, as you feed him, let him move, if released he will consume.

The Purple—Not much is known, but he wants destruction—meaning his freedom brings the end of times, tucked in West Virginia's endless mines.

The Red/Eternal known as Kevik. His power enslaves those who lack. Granted to by the eclipse. He will find you at your weakest, killing you from within. His cult awaits within the depths. Find them and wait for the eclipse. A vessel is all that's needed.

The Yellow—the king awaits, even Chambers made his acquaintance. He fills you with a dread of fear, madness washing over you as you stop caring. He will kill you just for daring. Yet with the right will and might, his strength will fill you with eternal life.

The Dark—the last that I know. Death himself will find you though, everyone must answer to him, as he consumes the souls as they have been. Filled with no Malice, he just exists, to create a single sound from the rest.

That came out of me in a way I never expected. Poor Easton, Poe, Chambers, I hear there is a man named Howard who is dancing with the entities as well. This is evil, and I guess at this point I have been tricked. Grandson—do not do it, yes, I found a new wife, and life, but Tootsie consumed it all. Simon, you shouldn't have followed my path. You have damned yourself.

November 24th, 1972

Simon jumped. The writing was coming on its own now. As if someone was just beneath the skin of the paper or writing on the other side.

I know you tried as I did. To bring back those you loved. In a way I think I did, as my heart tells me the soul of my son is within you. It is the voice of the Crawler leading you away from the light I tried to guide you to. You killed my hometown, you can't proceed. Or maybe it was the purple, or something from in between, either way we were deceived they will never—

Simon slammed the book shut. How much of the book had been written after his first reading. Could it be possible that the old ones have been manipulating him, manipulating the book? Was it even his grandfather's writings? Was it anything worthwhile, or were they all manipulating him in their own ways?

Caeben has indeed done such a thing. He took Three Forks without you having a full idea, granted it may take fifty or more years. As has the purple. They all have their ideas, but I can help you. I know the Purple visited, saying he can revive as well, but that power does not belong to the Caeben or the Purple. It is only I, Daemon, who can do what must be done, except at a cost.

Deep green eyes filled Simon's mind, he wanted to vomit at the sight.

People say they know about me, but your cult can only go so far. There are so many entities, and I can do it all.

A fog surrounded me, caressing my body. Filling me with hope, and love.

"What can I do?"

The voice spoke but was almost unable to be heard. *Find me in San.* And it was gone.

San Francisco. That's what it had to mean, right?

Lord, he needed to save her. To bring her back. Even if it is the same trap his grandfather fell into. Even if they were lies that were written within his book. He needed to win, to save her... even if she might be upset about their sons. But he can bring them back too. Yes, of course, that is such a simple sense.

Simon smiled as he walked out of the hotel to his truck. It was going to be a heck of a trip.

He jumped in the truck with one thing on his mind, San Francisco.

No, a voice screamed in his mind. But the Purple fucker could shove it for now. He needed to finish what his grandpa had started, and he would do anything to do that. He mashed the accelerator and sped away on 58, heading for Jenkins. His heart was full again with hope and lust. He would see her again, and if anyone got in his way, they would die. The Damned would rise, and there wasn't a damn thing the Swords or anyone else could do about it.

About the Author

K. L. Patrick is a writer, philosopher, and playwright. Born in the Blue Ridge Mountains of Virginia, his work is focused mainly in Appalachia and the horrors that can lie in the unknown regions of the mountains.

He has a bachelor's degree in theatre, with his first play debuting next summer. Before pursuing writing, he channeled his creative energies through music and theatre. Having worked on over ninety plays, in every role, from director to lighting designer, to actor.

He is the author of The Disappearing of Three Forks, which was an Amazon #1 new release within its first week out. He lives in the Appalachian Mountains outside of Roanoke, Virginia, with his five Guinea Pigs and three cats.

Scan to Follow on Facebook for all updates.

Also By

Also by K.L. Patrick

The Disappearing of Three Forks

The Red Mirror: A Short Story

The Horror Zine Magazine Spring 2025

In The Dark, They Wait